THAT TIME IN VENICE

BOOK 6 OF THE LOVE UNEXPECTED SERIES

DELANEY DIAMOND

D1160802

That Time in Venice
Copyright © 2017 by Delaney Diamond
Garden Avenue Press
Atlanta, Georgia
ISBN: 978-1-940636-46-7

PROLOGUE

Venice

*A*nika woke up wedged against Reed. With her head resting on his shoulder and his strong arms around her, she could almost believe their stilted conversation the night before had been a bad dream. She'd known their time together wouldn't last forever, but found it hard to let go.

She lay quietly, basking in the heat of his skin, dreading the moment he said goodbye.

"Good morning," Reed croaked.

She rolled away from him without a word, and he sat up on the side of the bed. The muscles of his back were within touching distance, but she didn't touch, no matter how much she ached for the contact. He was leaving today, and the distance between them grew wider with each passing minute.

Don't embarrass yourself. It's over. It was fun while it lasted.

They dressed quietly, pulling on jeans and tops, their movements robotic and stiff. While Anika brushed her hair, she watched Reed in the mirror. He hunted for his shoes, finding one next to the wall and the other under the bed. Their lovemaking had been particularly feverish last night, their clothes strewn across the room with a level of careless-ness and impatience before unseen.

By the time she finished pinning up her hair, he was on his feet. Today he left for Turin and would then travel to France. She'd offered him an extra night in her room, but he claimed to be on a tight schedule.

They stood across the room from each other, and she real-ized she couldn't let him go without making one last effort to turn the past few days into something more than a cheap fling.

"We um, we could exchange numbers. You know, to keep in touch. Maybe we could hang out once you're back in the States."

Reed rubbed the back of his neck, barely making eye contact. "I'm moving to New York when I get back. I already have a job lined up at the accounting firm where I interned." He sighed. "Listen, it's better this way."

"So this is it?" It couldn't be. The thought of never seeing him again sent a frisson of pain straight to her heart.

"We had fun, and I think it's best if what happened here...stayed here."

She pressed her trembling lips together, praying he didn't notice how her eyes filled with tears. She had been fooled. This was the real Reed. A player, a drifter with a devil-may-care attitude. A man who definitely didn't care about her.

He cursed and shoved long fingers through his messy curls. "I didn't mean to hurt you, Anika."

She kept balance to her voice. "I'm not hurt. We had a good time, and now it's at an end. I'm fine. You're fine. You never made me any promises." Her body had never been under this type of stress before. Pain twisted her insides tighter than nautical rope.

He took a step toward her, his face fixed in a piteous expression. "Anika...you deserve the ideal. A fairytale. I'm

2

not the person to give it to you. I'm not a prince. You should forget about me."

Impossible, but she lifted her chin and glared at him. "You're right. You're no prince." Her voice shook, and she stared at the ground as tears swelled anew in her eyes. "Go. Please."

He didn't leave as she asked, and she continued to stare at the tan and brown carpet. Surely he'd be kind enough to get out so she could grieve in private.

"You're a great girl, Anika. Someone will appreciate you one of these days."

His words only sharpened the pain. She didn't care about a potential man from the future. In a short period of time, she'd fallen for him, Reed Stewart, and banal comments about what the future held couldn't neutralize the agonizing emptiness that stretched out before her.

She memorized every detail of his features. His height, his broad shoulders and fit body beneath the dark T-shirt and jeans, the curls she'd grown so accustomed to running her fingers through, the shadow of hair on his jaw, and the sorrow in his clear blue eyes. He was so much more than she had ever dared to dream she could have.

"I know," she whispered.

Silence filled the room.

"Anika."

"Just *go*, Reed." She pleaded now, begging for a reprieve.

He swallowed hard and then left.

The minute the door closed, Anika flung herself onto the bed. She'd been broken down and emptied of everything but the pain of losing him. Sobbing, she pressed her face into the pillow where he'd lain. The scent of him still lingered on the fabric. A scent she would not soon forget.

CHAPTER 1

"Good morning," Anika Taylor sang at the receptionist as she walked into Davenport Design Studio. She dropped her umbrella in the container at the front door.

Jasmine, her shoulder length dark hair flipped up at the ends, turned away from the printer behind her desk and shoved a pair of horn-rimmed glasses higher on her broad nose. "What are you so happy about on a rainy Monday morning?"

"I'm happy to be alive. Do I need any other reason?"

"Hmmm…you must have had a great date this weekend."

"Sadly, I didn't." Anika rolled her eyes, and her coworker laughed.

Online dating had been a bust so far. She tended to date older men, often twice her age. They were mature and well-established, and most of them didn't play games. That wasn't the case with this weekend's bachelor. Men were men whatever their age, it turned out.

Friday, her second date with an investment banker went downhill fast, starting with him complaining about how he believed his children—both in college—were taking advantage of his generosity. The night ended on a sour note when he tried to guilt her into bed because he'd taken her out for an expensive meal. She couldn't believe a man his age believed a prix-fixe meal that totaled in the low three-digits warranted her taking her clothes off. Whatever happened to companionship? Getting to know someone?

Before sliding behind the wheel of her own vehicle, Anika had handed him a hundred-dollar bill to cover her dinner and instructed him to lose her number.

A sly smile slid across her lips. "You'll never guess what I got." With exaggerated slowness, she pulled a Starbucks sack from her large purse and placed it gently on the desk.

Jasmine's eyes widened and she breathed the next words. "You. Did. Not."

"It was the last one."

Jasmine groaned. "You're such a bad influence. You know I can't eat whatever I want like you do."

Anika eyed her coworker's frame. Jasmine was solid and curvy, but not overweight. "Please, you can afford to cheat every now and again."

With that little encouragement, Jasmine snatched up the sack containing the chocolate croissant and opened it. She sniffed the contents, taking a prolonged drag. "You had them warm it for me." Her grateful eyes met Anika's.

"Of course. Had them do the same for me." She patted the leather bag on her shoulder, indicating one of the tasty pastries was in there for her, too. "Break room in five minutes?"

Jasmine's brow wrinkled. "We won't be able to."

"Why not?"

They always enjoyed their chocolate croissants together over cups of steaming black coffee while they gossiped in the break room. On a rainy Monday morning, the phones wouldn't be ringing much, and anyway, Jasmine could have calls rolled to the answering service while they took the short break.

"Laura has a new client coming in today and she wants you in on the meeting. He'll be here at eight thirty, so you better hurry."

"Why did she schedule a meeting so early?" Anika grumbled.

"He's a referral from Judge Evers, and you know Laura wants to keep her happy because it means more prestigious referrals."

"Oh, that explains it."

Every referral from the judge had turned into more referrals as the firm's name was shared among a growing list of high-end clients. They couldn't buy that type of publicity. And, Laura had talked to Anika about buying a minority stake in the company so she could take more time off in the future. This would be an opportunity for Anika to shine again.

"Oh well, I guess I'll have my croissant later. Much later."

Jasmine clutched the papers to her chest and bit the corner of her bottom lip. "Don't be too upset. Judge Evers's secretary says the new client isn't bad on the eyes."

Anika arched a brow in interest. "Oh yeah?"

"Mhmm."

"I'll see for myself and we can discuss him later."

The two women giggled and Anika walked away.

Davenport Design Studio was an interior design firm located in Atlanta and specializing in residential interiors. The offices of the large converted house in Buckhead contained five designers, two project managers, supporting staff, interns, and Laura Davenport, the woman at the helm of the successful company.

Anika climbed the stairs to the second floor offices, her heels barely making a sound because of the burgundy carpet runner. Walking briskly down the hall, she waved to other members of the team, including another good work friend named Edgar, one of the project managers. She entered her office near the end of the hall and with a quick flip of a switch, light bounced off the yellow walls, casting a warm glow on the drafting table near the window and across her neat desk.

With no time to dally because she knew Laura was waiting, she hung her coat on the rack in the corner, dropped her large bag in the bottom drawer of her desk, and then wrote a quick to-do list of tasks that needed completing after the meeting. Everyone else in the office used tablets or other electronic devices to take notes and keep up with their schedules, but she preferred the old school options—notebooks to take notes and keeping up with her calendar in a pastel blue and pink planner. After a quick text to one of the interns, reminding him to stop by a local showroom to take photos of several pieces she was considering for a staging project later, Anika scraped up her pen and notepad and hurried back down the stairs to Laura's office on the first floor.

Behind the frosted glass covering the door, she made out the singular shape of her boss. Two quick knocks and Laura called her in.

She sat behind her desk, an abundance of hairspray making her platinum blonde hair an unmoving helmet. Her makeup, jewelry, and clothing were understated but elegant.

"Good morning."

"Anika, honey," Laura said in her husky Southern drawl. "I'm so glad you're here. Have a seat." She waved Anika into the chair opposite the desk. "Judge Evers has once again sung our praises and sent us a referral, but I haven't had time to get much information. Her secretary called late yesterday and set everything up. The judge didn't ask for you by name, but she did mention she wanted the same designer who'd done such a wonderful job on Representative Johnson's surprise birthday gift for his daughter. You really did do a marvelous job. You breathed new life into that place."

"Thank you." Laura did not hand out compliments often, so Anika knew the words were not only sincere, but she must have really done one hell of a job.

"Obviously, this new client takes priority. You know we want to keep the judge happy."

"Yes, I do."

"Here's what I know." Laura spoke with her hands a lot, gesturing, pointing, and spreading her fingers. "He's a manager with the accounting firm Continuum, and they transferred him to the Atlanta area. He hasn't lived here long but bought his house a few months ago and wants to redo the interior."

"Sounds easy enough. Only redecorating?" The firm offered redecorating and remodeling services.

"That's what I understand, but of course once you get over there, you'll be better able to make an assessment." Laura leaned forward. "If you do a good job on this, Anika, we'll work something out on the ownership front. I'd love to take some time off. My husband is retiring soon and I'm not getting any younger." She laughed.

A long time ago Laura had embraced the decision to not have children. Refusing to use the word childless, she extolled the positives of being child*free*—freedom to do whatever she wanted when she wanted with more disposable income. On more than one occasion she'd said she didn't think her business would have grown the way it did if she and her husband had had children. And soon she'd be using that disposable income to do more traveling and engage in more leisure activities.

Laura's voice dropped. "I trust you, and if you're interested, I'm willing to give you a leadership role."

This was the opportunity she'd been waiting for. Laura was no longer hinting. That was the second time in the conversation she'd flat out made her intentions known. "I'm very interested, and I would be honored."

As Laura prepared to reply, a knock sounded on the door and Jasmine poked her head in. "Mr. Stewart is here. Should I bring him in or wait a few minutes?"

"Oh my, he's early." Laura glanced at her watch. "Go ahead and bring him in, darling. We're ready."

Jasmine disappeared, and only moments later the door was reopened.

Laura came to her feet and extended her hand.

Anika stood as well and faced the newcomer, freezing when her gaze landed on the man who'd entered, her eyes widening fractionally when they connected with blue ones.

"Good morning, Mr. Stewart. I'm Laura Davenport, and this is—"

"Reed?" Anika said in quiet shock.

He stared back, the expression of surprise on his face undoubtedly reflected on hers.

What were the chances? She hadn't seen him in seven years. She'd been twenty-one and had completed her junior year in college. He'd just graduated.

Anika had worked with him in the dining hall, and hadn't known him well, but had known *of* him. Popular on campus, Reed had a reputation for having a laid back attitude and carefree demeanor. But behind the lazy smile and casual clothes had lurked a well-honed body of firm muscle. She'd seen for herself when he played Frisbee on the quad or rolled up his sleeves to empty heavy containers at the dining hall. He played baseball, had been the president of his fraternity, and garnered quite a reputation with the coeds.

By chance, she'd gotten to know him very well, far away from everything and everyone they were familiar with. Even as her heart clenched at the memory of what they'd shared, Anika catalogued his appearance. Time had been good to him. His black curly hair was cut shorter than in the past but was just as thick and lustrous, and his eyes remained on her with the same intense, assessing stare.

He seemed taller, but she knew that couldn't be right. Perhaps because years ago he'd been comfortable wearing jeans and T-shirts, while today he oozed style and polish and appeared a little imposing in all black—black jacket, black shirt, black slacks.

Damn. He looked so...*good*.

Hair covered his chin and jaw, enough scruff to tickle and tease, but not enough to bother or annoy. She knew the sensation well—across the tips of her breasts as he sucked her nipples, and down her spine to the small of her back. His hands and lips had been *everywhere* on her body. For months after they'd parted ways, she'd woken up at odd times of the night, aching for him.

"Anika."

Her body reacted to the warm sound of his voice, the low, sexy sound echoing inside of her. Her nipples tightened. Her pulse jumped. Her entire being quivered, recognizing the voice of the man who'd given her exquisite memories one summer a long time ago.

"Y-you live here now?" Anika asked.

He nodded. "I moved from New York six months ago."

Laura glanced from one to the other. "So the two of you know each other?" she asked slowly.

Anika swallowed. "We—we haven't seen each other in a long time. Years. Not since..."

Reed's jaw tightened at the unspoken words left dangling in the air. His jaw had often tightened under the weight of intense emotion—anger, sadness, ecstasy. Suddenly, the memories of fierce passion, inexhaustible and relentless, evoked heat in her insides.

Her mind flashed back to heated whispers, her back pressed against a hard wall, and his hands beneath her skirt. His driving thrusts as he pinned her beneath him in bed, their

11

hearts beating rapidly in synch, and their sweat-sprinkled bodies wrapped around each other during what had been, without a doubt, the best week of her life. An unbelievable, breathtaking six days in Italy.

Seven years, and she'd never forgotten that trip—or *him*.

"That time in Venice," he finished for her.

Anika swallowed again, forcing back the constriction in her throat. What they'd shared had been so unexpected, starting out innocently enough before snowballing into an avalanche of emotion that almost broke her.

"Yeah," she whispered. "Not since Venice."

CHAPTER 2

*A*nika Taylor. What were the chances?

"Is the fact that the two of you know each other good or bad?" Laura's eyes flicked at them from beneath a wrinkled brow.

"Um…" Anika hedged, at the same time Reed said, "Good."

Laura raised an eyebrow, and Anika shot a glance at him.

"I don't have a problem with us working together, do you?" he asked.

"I'm fine if you're fine." She smiled, but the expression in her eyes didn't match the upward tilt of her mouth.

"I'm absolutely fine."

"Then we're both fine," Anika said.

They stared at each other.

"Good!" Laura pressed her hands together. "Please, have a seat."

Reed waited for both ladies to sit before lowering into the chair beside Anika. The side of his body closest to her remained tense. The muscles in his right arm contracted, his neck uncomfortably stiff and tight.

"I don't know how much you know about us, but I

founded this firm twenty-three years ago on a shoestring budget, with a loan from my daddy, and a whole lotta prayer."

Reed smiled. While some southerners tried to lose their accents, Laura clearly embraced hers. He enjoyed listening to her speak. Though not as much as Anika.

"We've grown into the company you see today. Our reputation is very important to us, and we've built this firm by taking good care of our clients. People like you. We specialize in residential decor. No project is too small. No project is too big. Renovations, redesign—you name it, we do it. Now"— she clasped her hands together on the desk—"tell us about this house you bought."

"Well, it's a great place. Four bedrooms, living room, den off the kitchen, and a spacious deck out back that runs the full length of the house. A husband and wife lived there before me and took good care of the place, but it does need some updating—except in the kitchen. Lucky for me, the wife was a Food Network fan who fancied herself an amateur chef, so that at least is in pristine condition. I'd like to put some color on the walls, maybe add new light fixtures. I don't know much about that type of thing." He shrugged and laughed, glancing at Anika, whose expression remained neutral. "I need new furniture, too, but I don't know the first thing about putting colors together. My old place was a one-bedroom apartment with only a living room. So as you can imagine, I need the works."

Laura nodded her understanding. "Rest assured we're ready and able to handle all of your project's needs. Anika is my very best designer. If anyone can transform your home into whatever you desire, she's the one to do it. I know you'll be very satisfied with her."

From the corner of his eye, he thought he saw Anika stiffen. His own body tightened. He had been very satisfied with her in the past. Very satisfied indeed.

Laura continued. "Anika will start with an initial consultation in your home—no obligation, of course—which will allow her to see the scope of the project and get a sense of your style. Then she'll put together some initial ideas. You'll both discuss options until you're absolutely satisfied with the design plan. By the way, is there a Mrs. Stewart?"

"No, but there's a Miss Stewart. I have a daughter."

"You have a daughter?" Anika's voice reeked with shock.

Laura and Reed glanced at her.

"I'm surprised, that's all," she said.

"She lives with me full-time and is very opinionated about the design of her new room. Her current obsession is butterflies, which she wants incorporated into the design. I'm open to just about anything, within reason."

"We can certainly handle that. So aside from that bedroom, it sounds as if you'll be able to make the final decisions." Laura smiled pleasantly. "What we'll do next is have Anika take you to her office to set up a time for that consultation. I want to assure you that we take customer service very seriously. It's our honor to be invited into your home, and we don't take that privilege lightly. Before I let Anika take you away, do you have any questions for me, Mr. Stewart?"

"Only one. Will you promise to call me Reed and not Mr. Stewart? Mr. Stewart sounds way too formal." He flashed his most charming grin, which he'd used for years to seduce women and strip them of their inhibitions.

Laura blushed and laughed. "Well of course, but you must call me Laura. And while I have every confidence that Anika will take good care of you, should you have any problems at all, *please* feel free to contact me directly. Here is my card with my direct extension." She handed it over. "We take good care of all our clients, but Judge Evers has been such a good friend to our firm—sending us lovely people such as yourself—we want you to be happy so that she doesn't regret referring you to us."

"I will definitely do that, Laura. But I have no concerns whatsoever. Davenport Design Studio has a stellar reputation, and I'm sure Judge Evers wouldn't have given me your name if she wasn't satisfied with your work and the great job you've done for her friends."

Laura beamed.

They all stood, and he shook Laura's hand, making sure to maintain eye contact and send another smile her way. "It was a pleasure."

"The pleasure was all mine, Reed," Laura drawled, a spark of interest emerging in the depths of her eyes.

Anika cleared her throat. "My office is upstairs. Follow me, please."

Reed pulled up the rear as Anika walked down the hall and up the stairs toward her office. He'd been completely unprepared for her appearance, which had left him temporarily speechless. She was even prettier than he remembered, captivating—not unlike the very first time he spotted her as a new hire going through orientation, chewing on the end of a pen and occasionally taking what appeared to be detailed notes in a small spiral bound pad.

As she walked ahead of him into her office, his gaze outlined her torso. Her body was fuller. Riper. The feminine curve of her waist and hips were outlined by the high-waisted tan pants and cream-colored blouse that played well against her light brown skin. Gold heels added a few inches to her frame, bringing her little more than up to the tip of his nose. Her dark hair, highlighted with golden-blonde and framing her heart-shaped face, swept past her neck and slid across her shoulders in a smooth sweep of shiny strands.

Inside her office he shut the door, inhaling the scent of citrus and ginger, a subtle but pleasing aroma that filled the room. This didn't surprise him at all. Anika was a girly girl, sugar and spice and all things nice. The kind who drew hearts over the letter "i" in her words and wore soft, flowing fabrics in pastel colors. Soft-spoken and friendly, she came across as a kitten, but oh man, in bed, the kitten turned into a tigress.

"This office suits you," Reed said, glancing around.

Framed quotes on the wall offered positive and inspirational remarks about life and love. Bright pink, orange, and gold-colored boxes sat on white shelves with knickknacks and books, arranged in such a way to be functional but also artistic. The rest of the room was decorated in a similar colorful fashion, with a drafting table and high-backed stool in front of it, photos on the wall depicting water colors of flowers and other plant life, and a small bookcase filled with pastel-colored three-inch binders behind her desk. Everything indicated the person who occupied this space contained a vibrant, vivacious personality.

Standing behind her desk, Anika opened a blue and pink planner and flipped through the pages. "Let's see, which day should I come by? I have—"

"It's quite a coincidence, isn't it? Running into each other?"

"Yes, quite a coincidence." She kept her attention on the planner. "I can meet with you on Wednesday or Thursday, if you're free. My schedule is wide open in the afternoon on both those days."

He couldn't stop staring at her. "How have you been?"

Her gaze lifted to his face. "Excuse me?"

"How have you been?"

He wanted to know everything. What had she been doing in the intervening years? Where did she live? How long had she been working in interior design? Was she seeing anyone or married? His gaze dropped to her left hand, and his brain became drenched in unexpected relief when he saw her bare fingers.

He hadn't been able to forget Anika and almost immediately regretted not staying in touch. If he had the opportunity to relive their last moments together, he'd handle the separation differently. Hell, maybe he wouldn't have left at all. He'd never regretted anything the way he regretted leaving her that day. Maybe—just maybe, fate was giving him another chance.

"I'm okay. Nothing special going on with me." She seemed guarded, her answer purposely vague.

"I seriously doubt that. Do you enjoy your job?"

"Yes."

The clipped response didn't deter him. "Have you lived anywhere else?"

"No, but I don't think I could. I love my city." She shrugged.

"No shame in that."

She focused on the planner again. "What's your schedule like later this week?"

"Slow down. I want to talk and catch up a little."

"Why?"

The question caught him off guard. "What do you mean, why? Because…"

"Because what? I have to do a good job."

"I understand, and I don't doubt that you will, but…" He blew out a frustrated breath of air. He was so desperate to talk to her and find out how she'd been, while she seemed completely uninterested in engaging in any kind of small talk. "Would it hurt to take a few minutes to catch up?"

"I'm extremely busy. As you can see." She gestured toward her desk, the neat and orderly appearance doing nothing to substantiate the claim.

"Why are you being so cold?"

"I'm sorry, were you expecting a hug and a kiss?"

He didn't think it was possible, but the temperature in the room plunged below zero. Her dark brown eyes, devoid of emotion, seemed to look through him. He didn't know what he was expecting, but it certainly wasn't this. "No. Of course not." He'd expected—hoped, he'd see a glimpse of the woman he'd spent time with in Italy. They'd joked around, seen the sights together, and made love like there was no tomorrow. Swallowing his pride, he answered the almost forgotten question. "I work from home a few days a week. How about Wednesday?"

A slender, light brown finger scrolled down the page. "One o'clock okay?"

"That's good for me," he said, voice as clipped and devoid of emotion as hers.

Anika wrote in the planner, capped her pen, and set it on the desk. She smiled brightly, as though nothing was amiss. He began to wonder if he were crazy.

"I have a little homework assignment for you. Go to the ideas tab on our website and look at the different decorating styles—eclectic, traditional, contemporary, etcetera—and give some thought to what you think your style is. We can talk in more detail when I see you on Wednesday, but I want you to examine the photos so we can discuss which one you find yourself gravitating toward. Also, think about the changes you want to make, the furniture you want to keep, do you want to start from scratch with a clean slate—that kind of thing. Don't feel pressured to make any decisions. I only want you thinking about these things so we have a starting point. Okay?"

Her aloofness irritated him. She really was treating him like any old customer. As if they didn't spend almost every minute of every day together for six straight days. As if they hadn't been lovers. As if she hadn't clawed his ass and gasped his name as she came.

"I can do that."

"We're all set. Do you have any questions for me?"

"Small world, isn't it?" He couldn't help pressing forward, demanding a response.

She averted her eyes to the desktop. "Very."

"I'm looking forward to working with you." Reed

19

extended his hand, and for a split second thought she wouldn't take it, but then she clasped his larger hand in her smaller one.

Her soft skin sent a zing of electricity through his veins. As his fingers tightened fractionally around hers, her full lips parted slightly. No sound came out, but his chest tightened with the memory of those lips against his, and he was glad for the glass and wood desk between them. Otherwise, he might have done something irrational, such as pull her in for a quick taste.

Anika tugged away her hand, clenching it into a fist at her side. "I'll see you on Wednesday." She kept her face neutral, but he didn't miss the underlying tremble in her voice. The fire was still there, waiting to consume them.

"I'll see you then."

Reed walked out of the office, letting the door swing close behind him. He flexed his tingling hand.

Those brief moments alone with Anika reminded him of what could have been, if he hadn't been a dumb twenty-two-year-old, afraid to take a chance. But he was older now.

And much, much wiser.

CHAPTER 3

*A*nika peered through the blinds of her second floor window as Reed took confident, long-legged strides to a navy blue Tahoe in the parking lot. The rain had stopped, but dark clouds remained in the sky, promising more showers later in the day.

He climbed his fit body into the vehicle and drove away, and her gaze followed the entire time until he turned onto the main road. Only then could she breathe easier.

"Knock, knock." Jasmine stood in the doorway holding a rectangular box. "This came for you. I figured you'd want it right away."

"Is that the new vase for the Winthrops?"

"I believe so."

"Thank goodness." The Winthrops were a wealthy and needy client. She'd been working with them for months, and as with all events associated with Murphy's Law, the neediest client encountered the most problems during a redesign.

Jasmine set the box on the desk and Anika cut it open. She removed the stuffing and held the multi-colored Chinese vase up to the light, twisting and turning to see it from all angles.

The last vase had arrived with two chips, one at the lip and the other at the base. This one was in pristine condition.

"Perfect." She could finally consider the redesign complete.

"You want me to have one of the interns run the vase over to the Winthrops?"

"No, I'll do it." They'd had so many problems, she wanted to personally deliver this last item and make sure the family was happy. "But do me a favor and call Mrs. Winthrop, and let her know I'm on my way. I'm going over there now."

Anika stuffed the packing material and vase back into the box and grabbed her coat and purse.

"Sooo, are you going to keep me in suspense? What do you think?"

"About what?" Anika asked.

Jasmine fisted a hand on her hip. "Don't be coy. What do you think of our new client?"

Anika slipped her arms through the sleeves of her coat. "Actually, I know him."

"Oh really? How do you know him?"

"We went to Georgia State together." Anika flung her purse over her shoulder and picked up the box, hugging it to her torso.

"So he's an old college friend?"

"Not a friend, really. More of an acquaintance. Our work-study assignment was in the dining hall. We haven't seen each other in years, though." She'd never told anyone the whole story about her trip to Venice. Even her cousin Ronnie only knew bits and pieces and not all the details.

"What a coincidence," Jasmine said.

"Mhmm. See you later." She hurried out to avoid discussing Reed any further. She worried Jasmine would pick up on her discomfort.

Downstairs, Anika picked up her umbrella at the door and walked to the car.

There are no coincidences. That's what her mother always said, a firm believer in "everything happens for a reason." No matter how delicate or painful or damaging a circumstance, her mother found a way to spin it positively, and she'd influenced Anika's viewpoints over the years.

Seven years ago, Anika ran into Reed thousands of miles away from their campus. Seeing a familiar face—even if it belonged to Reed Stewart—had brightened what could have been a mediocre vacation all by herself.

* * *

Venice

She was actually in Venice!

Anika couldn't stop smiling as she leaned on the railing of the water taxi, cruising down the Grand Canal. All of her senses worked overtime. A temperate breeze wafted through her hair and across her skin, cooling her body beneath the sun's warm rays. Taking a deep breath, she inhaled the fresh air mingled with the scent of briny, teal-colored water and let her gaze encompass all the boats gliding in the water around them. Lifting her camera, she snapped a photo of the seascape spread out before her. Then took additional pictures of the buildings on either side of the canal, a colorful display that showcased the city's Byzantine and Islamic architectural influences.

They stopped at the water landing of Hotel Bonvecchiati, a renovated palazzo built in 1790. The hotel was located in the heart of Venice and a three-minute walk to the Piazza San Marco and the Basilica of San Marco, popular tourist stops in the city center.

The driver, a lean Italian wearing sunglasses, helped Anika descend the boat along with the other passengers. She blushed when he kissed the back of her hand. His gentle flirtation was just what she needed to soothe the painful reason for her trip to Italy.

She dragged her rolling suitcase into the lobby and checked in, and within half an hour had dropped her luggage in the room, pulled her hair into a ponytail, and made her way back downstairs.

Standing in front of the hotel, she studied a street map. Her first trip abroad by herself, and all of a sudden the magnitude of the experience overwhelmed her. Originally she'd planned to go with the flow of the vacation, but now she wasn't so sure that was a good idea. She needed a plan, but what should she do first? She flipped open one of a handful of brochures. Go to the piazza now or a cafe for a bite to eat? And where was a good place to eat?

She should ask the concierge for advice. She turned in the direction of the hotel with every intention of doing that, when a familiar voice arrested her steps.

"Well, well, well. What have we here?"

A faint tingle of apprehension dotted her shoulder blades. All the way from Georgia to Venice, and she runs into *him*.

Reed Stewart stood with a little smile twisting up one corner of his mouth, a Georgia State baseball cap pulled low on his head. Last time she'd seen him was at a party, holding a half-empty beer bottle and grinding on a brunette in a corner.

"Hey," she said dryly, immediately annoyed. She'd had the misfortune of working with Reed in the school dining hall, and he'd been nothing but a pain in the rear. He didn't take his job seriously and spent way too much time flirting with the female students and staff.

Despite all that, he had a magnetic personality—enough so that she avoided him whenever possible. She became uneasy around him but couldn't put her finger on the exact reason why.

"What are you doing in Venice, Anika Taylor?"

"Summer vacation." She kept her answer short and scanned the brochure about moped tours, hoping he'd take the hint and leave her alone.

He didn't. He surveyed her from his superior height. "Are you here by yourself?"

"What's it to you?"

"Why so touchy, princess?"

His grin annoyed her. She suspected that he was laughing at her. The word princess annoyed her, too, because she had the impression it was by no means a compliment.

"I'm not being touchy. I just don't know why you need that information."

"I'm making conversation. I'm here by myself. See how easy that was? How about you? Are you here by yourself?"

He'd managed to make her feel like she was overreacting. "Yes."

"No friends? No family?"

"No. Only me. That's what by myself means."

His eyebrows lifted.

"Why did you do that?" Anika asked.

"Do what?"

"Act surprised."

"I don't know, I figured you'd be here with someone." He folded his arms across his chest, giving added definition to the pectorals under the cotton shirt.

Anika kept her gaze up so she wouldn't stare. "Are you saying I don't seem like the type to solo travel?"

He shrugged one shoulder. "Sorry, you don't."

Her mouth fell open.

"Come on, you know I'm right. I can't believe your boyfriend let you come on this trip alone. What's his name again? Is it Emmett?"

"Emerson."

"That's right. Emerson."

"For your information, he didn't *let* me do anything. I do what I want."

She hid her pain behind a rebellious attitude, but the truth was, Emerson was supposed to accompany her on this trip. They'd planned a romantic end of school year getaway for the two of them, but only a few days ago, he'd broken up with her, forcing her to take the trip alone. But that was none of Reed's business.

"You do what you want, huh? You're just full of surprises." The slow drawl and the way his eyes slowly scrolled down her pink halter to her purple and pink Capri pants made Anika a little self-conscious.

The hairs on the back of her neck tingled, and she straightened her spine. She'd caught him watching her in the same way before, in a bold and assessing manner. The first time she'd thought it was her imagination, but then she'd caught his eyes on her one night while they closed down the salad bar. He made her very conscious of her own movements. When her boyfriend came around, Reed was friendly enough, but it didn't keep him from that unnerving silent observation when they were alone.

"How long are you here for?" she asked, in an effort to switch the topic of conversation away from her.

He stepped out of the way of a woman entering the hotel. "I came in yesterday, and I'm staying until the end of the week. I'm traveling through Europe before I have to deal with the responsibilities of getting a job and all that other adult stuff."

Anika played with her bag strap, not knowing what else to say. She thought about the coming changes, as well. One more year and she'd be on the hunt for a job and an apartment.

"If you want to hang out, let me know. We could keep each other company," Reed said.

Anika blinked. The invitation took her by surprise. "I don't think you'd want to do the same things I do," she said.

"How do you know?" He tilted his head at her, that little smile making another appearance.

"Are you interested in glass blowing, for instance? That's on my list of things to do."

"Oh." He rubbed a hand across his clean-shaven jaw. "Glassblowing, huh?"

He seemed to give the idea such serious thought, she couldn't help but laugh. "That's what I thought."

"No, wait a minute now. Actually, that sounds fascinating. I'm sure it's really cool, and it's one of the things to do while here, right? We could go to one of the factories on Murano."

"You know about that?"

"Sure I do. Count me in."

Apparently, Reed was full of surprises, too.

"Really?"

"Uh-huh. I'm not just saying that."

"Okay, cool." She smiled. "So, what's on your agenda for the trip?"

He hooked his thumbs into the loops of his jeans. "Playing it by ear. My goal is to stay out of trouble."

"Is that even possible?"

He quirked a brow at her. "Yes, it's possible, but not probable. Trouble seems to follow me wherever I go." He grinned. He had a sexy mouth. A thin upper lip but a full lower one that looked kissably soft.

Crap. Where did that come from?

Anika cleared her throat. "I'm staying out of trouble while I'm here."

He contemplated her for long seconds. "You're not the type to get into trouble anyway."

"What does that mean?" Anika asked, mildly offended.

He laughed softly. "I'm guessing you're a good girl, and there's nothing wrong with that, by the way."

"I am a good girl, but that doesn't mean I can't have fun, too."

"Come on. You probably have a super neat desk at home, and I bet Jake would have given you the employee of the month award every month, but that would have been embarrassing for the rest of us."

She blushed. Their boss had said something similar, remarking on her dependability when compared to the other student employees. Even though she knew he was baiting her, Anika rose to the challenge anyway. "Well, you're wrong. I love trouble. I court trouble."

"Is that right?" Amusement filled his blue eyes, and he rubbed his jaw. "We'll see about that."

Excitement inched down her spine. "Wait a minute, what did you have in mind?"

"Something other than glass-blowing, that's for sure." His eyes sparkled with mischief. "I promise not to overstep my bounds. I wouldn't want Emerson to kick my ass." He said it sarcastically, as if that would never happen.

"You don't have to worry about that," Anika muttered.

"Yeah, I know. So listen, have you eaten?"

"No, I haven't."

"Perfect, cause I'm starving, and yesterday I found this neat little place in a non-touristy part of the city. It's got great food, great wine, and cheap prices. You game?"

"I've never drunk before."

His eyebrows shot upward. "Never? But you're going to, right?"

"I don't know…"

"Come on, you're in Italy, princess. One glass. You've gotta taste the *vino*."

His enthusiasm was contagious. Anika laughed. "Okay, okay. I'm here for an adventure, so I'm open to anything."

"*Bene*." Reed winked, and in that moment, with the sun shining down on them on the cobblestoned streets in front of

Hotel Bonvecchiati, Anika saw him in a different light. Her stomach did a strange little twist, and she turned away from the appealing picture he made, his eyes lighting up, his even teeth revealed past lips pulled up at the corners in amusement.

"The restaurant is away from the city center, so we'll have to catch a water taxi. Let's go."

As Anika fell into step beside him, another strange little twist filtered into her stomach.

Reed Stewart was definitely trouble, but maybe a little trouble on this trip wouldn't be such a bad thing.

CHAPTER 4

*C*ould she do it? Could she work with Reed and not fall apart from the constant contact?

Of course. She was a professional and would impress Laura with the job she did for him, the same as with all her clients.

Anika parked at the curb outside his home. "This is it," she muttered.

The classic gray Tudor was nestled back from the street in a well-to-do area of Atlanta. She had no doubt why Reed settled in this part of town. The fun-loving bachelor he used to be would have never bought a house in this zip code, but Reed the single dad must have made a conscious decision to live near parks, schools with high test scores, and in a community where the neighbors probably all knew each other.

The quiet street held very little activity, except for a white minivan cruising by at an extremely slow pace. The driver squinted out the window as she checked the numbers on mailboxes.

Taking a deep breath, Anika strolled up the short walkway with a leather Burberry briefcase over her shoulder containing a laptop and other necessities. She couldn't do anything about the nervous tightening of her chest as she neared the steps that led to the double doors, so she steeled her nerves and prepared for the sight of Reed.

He appeared seconds after she rang the doorbell, once again breathtaking in a dark pullover and jeans. His curly hair was neatly combed, and the clothes covered him as if they'd been sewn on his body—fitted, but not tight. He made looking good so effortless.

"You found the house okay?"

She paid no attention to the warmth in his eyes or the sudden rise in her pulse rate. "Yes, it was easy to find."

"Come on in."

Stepping inside, she was immediately impressed by the interior. Reed had been right. The owners had taken good care of the place. Crown molding and gleaming hardwood in the front foyer lent an elegant introduction to the home.

The tour began right away, with Reed taking his time to show Anika throughout the first floor, pointing out rooms he wanted to paint and how the windows lacked any type of treatment. Each time he made a movement, her senses magnified the motion, so that she was acutely aware of the swing of his arm or the sound of his soft-soled shoes on the floors.

In the living room, she made the mistake of noticing his long fingers as he gestured to an empty wall, telling her he'd like a photo or a unique wall covering in the blank space. Anika *mhmmed* and nodded, but the movement of his fingers reminded her of how they'd trailed across her bare skin and how she'd come all over them as he plunged them two and three at a time inside her.

He was only inches away, within reach. She fanned her face with her notepad and walked into the center of the room to avoid looking at him.

The four bedrooms were upstairs, along with an office. They ended the tour with a return to the kitchen, where

Anika set up a makeshift desk at the bar, and Reed stood across from her.

"What do you think?" he asked.

"I have some ideas."

There were no pictures on the walls, and except for the living room, master bedroom, his daughter's room, and his office, the place was almost entirely unfurnished. During their walk-through she snapped photos and took measurements, but with the interior of the home such a blank canvas, her mind raced with possibilities—including knocking down the partial wall that separated the den from the kitchen. The change would open up the space and increase the light in both rooms, but she wondered if Reed would be open to such a drastic change.

"Did you get a chance to check out the website?" she asked, scrolling through the images on the digital camera.

"I did."

"So tell me about your vision." She snapped open her binder and pulled out a pen. "What would you say is your style?" This was the part clients struggled with, and it was her job to help them articulate what they wanted and narrow down the ideas.

Reed shrugged. "Simple."

"That wasn't one of the choices," she pointed out.

He laughed shortly. Amusement added a hint of light to his blue eyes. "Okay, what do you think?"

"I think…" The living room contained a large sectional, a TV, a sound system, and a worn love seat. A king bed sat in the middle of the master bedroom, with an old leather recliner in one corner whose condition suggested he'd had it for years. "You prefer comfortable furniture and functional pieces. You don't want a showroom. You're more suited to a place where you can come home and relax and feel as if you've escaped the day-to-day grind. A place you can actually live in."

Reed nodded thoughtfully. "You could say that. Right now my furniture is big and clunky. I suppose I could use a more feminine touch, but I don't want anything girly."

"A traditional aesthetic would suit you."

"Maybe. With consideration for my daughter, of course."

Anika made a note. She still couldn't believe Reed had a daughter and was raising her alone, no less. "How old is your daughter?"

"Four years old. I know I joked about her being opinionated, but it's very important to me that her room is exactly what she wants."

The tone of his voice held a gravity that made Anika look up. "I promise to do my best."

"Thanks. She's still a little fragile. Her mother passed away a year ago."

Anika gasped. "I'm so sorry. What happened?"

"Heart failure. I couldn't believe it, really. She was so healthy. She biked, ran—was all around athletic. One minute she was here, the next she was gone." He frowned, shaking his head.

It came as no surprise that Reed would fall for an athletic woman. In college he'd been rumored to be in relationships with several female athletes—one on the softball team and two swimmers. He himself had the muscular body of a man who probably worked out regularly. He used to be involved in intramural sports and had once shown her a photo of him and his father in California, standing on the beach with their surfboards.

"How is your daughter handling the loss of her mother?"

He rubbed a hand along the back of his neck, the frown deepening on his face. Anika had the sudden urge to throw her arms around him to ease his concerns. She'd never seen Reed like this. The worry etched in his face was unusual. She was accustomed to him being playful and laid back. "Most of the time Brielle—that's my daughter—is great. She's funny, playful, and a curious kid. But sometimes…sometimes she has bad days."

"That's understandable. It must have been hard for her to lose her mother so young."

He sighed, suddenly looking weary. "It was."

And how did Reed feel about his daughter's mother, she wondered, but didn't dare ask.

"I'll make sure she falls in love with her room." Anika asked a few more questions, delving deeper into his likes, dislikes, and color preferences. "I have all the information I need," she said finally. "I'll put together a few ideas and get back to you early next week." She gathered her belongings and zipped the briefcase closed.

"So how long have you been working at the design firm?"

"Quite a while. I worked as an intern for a different firm while I was in school and applied for a position at the Design Studio after graduation. Laura offered me a job right away. I've been there ever since. Six years now. How long have you been at Continuum?" She was interested to learn more about Reed and what he'd been up to in the intervening years but didn't want to appear too eager because she didn't want to encourage him.

"I have a similar story. I had a couple of summer internships with them, and when I graduated, they offered me a position in their New York office. Entry level stuff and a tough training ground, but I learned a helluva lot. Now I'm one of their managers."

"Do you miss New York?"

He rested a hip against the edge of the island. "Honestly, no. I enjoyed my time there, but moving here was the right decision. Recent developments have convinced me of that even more." Unblinking, he stared at her.

The temperature in the room went higher.

"Reed…"

"Are you seeing anyone?"

Anika clenched her fingers around the pen. "What are you doing? We agreed that what happened between us would remain there and now you want to ask me questions that are none of your business." She took a deep breath. "I don't even understand what happened. You cut me off. You didn't want to keep in touch. Did I do something wrong?" She'd promised herself not to go down this road, yet here she was, wanting—no, needing—to understand what had happened.

"*No*. It wasn't you. It was me."

"The old, it's-not-you-it's-me argument." She laughed softly, an empty, bitter sound.

"It's the truth. It's not just a line. I wasn't mentally ready to be in a relationship. That's no excuse, but it's the truth."

Anika remained silent, staring at the granite countertop.

"Running into you has reminded me of what I left. Of what we had." Reed came around to her side. "Are you seeing anyone?"

"I'm not answering your question."

"So you're not seeing anyone?" he pressed.

Her gaze shot up to his. "Why do you care?"

"Are you?" His determined gaze locked with hers.

Unbelievable. He wouldn't stop until she answered. Anika laughed softly and stared out the window at the deck. Finally, she responded. "I date."

"But you're not seeing anyone seriously?"

"Not at the moment."

"I find that hard to believe."

"Why? Different people are searching for different things."

"What are you searching for?"

"You're not my type, Reed."

"I don't believe that. Venice says different."

"I was hurting then. I needed to feel better, and you helped me feel better. I appreciated it so much, but that's all it was. We made each other feel better. I've accepted that."

"I thought that's all it was, too, until I saw you again.

Dammit, Anika, I know it was just six days, but I keep thinking about what happened between us. How perfect we were together. At least I thought we were perfect. Did you?" His eyes blazed with an earnest flame.

Shallow breaths left his lips, and her own breaths shortened at the memories. Touring the city on a scooter, an achy hunger filling her as she pressed her breasts against his firm back. Spending the night in deep conversation like an old couple, sharing a meal, licking the sticky sweetness of chocolate and sugar off each other's fingers. Waking up next to him each morning and burrowing deeper into his embrace as his hands caressed her hypersensitive breasts, belly, and hips. She'd never experienced anything like it before or since. Reed easily embodied all the traits of the men her love quotes were about.

"I did think we were perfect, but…"

"But what?"

She held her breath.

"I don't want to hurt you, Reed."

The tip of his finger touched her wrist and slowly dragged across her skin, leaving fire in the wake of his touch.

"Then don't."

Anika's inhibitions lowered as she drowned in the intensity of his eyes. Her heartbeat tripled in rate, the temptation to forgive and tell him everything—the ugly truth, her own fears—trembled on the tip of her lips. She opened her mouth to reply, but the slamming of the front door and the sound of a little girl's voice sidelined her answer.

"Daddy! Look what I got. Where are you?"

They both took a step back, and Anika clutched the briefcase to her chest, as if to stop the pain that blossomed behind her breasts.

"I'm in the kitchen," Reed called out. Regret filled his eyes and his jaw tightened.

A little girl dressed in jeans and a gray sweatshirt with

Butterfly Girl in a glitter design on the front raced into the kitchen carrying a plastic container of strawberries. She stopped abruptly when she saw Anika.

"Brielle, this is Miss Anika."

She sidled up to her father's thigh. "Hi, Miss Anika," Brielle said shyly, biting her bottom lip.

"Hi there," Anika greeted back.

"She's going to make our house and your room all pretty," Reed said.

"With butterflies?" Brielle asked hopefully, her eyes getting big and round.

"Oh, of course. Your daddy explained how important the butterflies are," Anika said.

Reed placed a hand on top of his daughter's coal black hair, styled on top of her head in a thick curly bun. She was an adorable little girl, with full cheeks, brown eyes and skin tinted a hint of color darker than his.

In addition to the shock that Reed was a father, Anika now added another unexpected development. Reed's daughter was mixed race.

CHAPTER 5

*A*nika heard the front door open and close again, and a tall, slender woman with pale skin and warm eyes entered the kitchen carrying canvas totes filled with groceries, one in each hand.

"Hello," she said, a pleasant smile on her face. Her short black hair was peppered with gray at the temples.

"Mrs. Miller, this is Anika. She's an interior designer. Anika, this is my housekeeper, Mrs. Miller. She's also Brielle's nanny. She keeps the house running in an orderly fashion and makes it all look easy." Reed took the bags and set them on the bar.

"That's not so hard when I have such lovely clients," Mrs. Miller said.

Her melodic Southern drawl had a soothing quality and inspired calm. Anika couldn't imagine her yelling and thought she had a future in radio if she ever wanted to switch careers.

"Miss Anika is going to make our new house look pretty," Brielle announced.

"Oh, wonderful. I can't wait to see what you do with the place."

"Mrs. Miller hopes that it's an improvement over what we have now," Reed said.

"It takes time. Can't rush these things, but this house is so much better than the old apartment."

"Oh yeah." Reed groaned. "Nice location, beautiful interior, but terrible management. Nothing worked in the apartment. If we plugged in more than one appliance to an outlet, the breaker tripped. And the plumbing was an absolute nightmare."

Mrs. Miller shook her head. "My goodness, how many times did the poor maintenance man have to stop in?"

"Too many. Now I know why I got such a good deal on the place."

"It was a blessing in disguise. The apartment was in such bad shape, it made you move quickly to buy a house, and you were fortunate to find this gem." Mrs. Miller patted Reed's arm in a maternal manner. "Brielle, you want to help me put away the groceries? Then we can wash the strawberries."

"Okay!" Brielle handed over the container to her nanny and upturned her face to Anika. "We wash the strawberries with vinegar and water so they last longer. Then I have strawberries as my snack *all* week." She seemed very excited about that, and skipped over to the refrigerator, where she and Mrs. Miller started placing items on the shelves.

"I better get going," Anika said. "I'll be in touch soon with some ideas for the house."

"I'll walk you out."

Anika didn't want him to but couldn't protest without drawing attention to herself. They walked in silence to her red sedan parked at the end of the driveway.

"She loves strawberries. Mrs. Miller taught me that vinegar trick. Brielle's grandmother in Dallas said Brielle was hooked on blueberries the same way at one time."

"Funny how when kids enjoy something, they focus on it so they can experience it over and over again." Anika placed her briefcase and purse on the passenger seat and shut the car door. "Well, I'll be in touch."

"Before you go...I want to talk about what happened before my daughter and Mrs. Miller showed up."

"I don't think that's a good idea."

"Why not?" A frown sat between his eyebrows.

"Reed, I don't know what you want me to say. Venice *was* wonderful, but we were young and had a great time. That's all it was."

"You're not even curious to see if our chemistry still exists?"

"I'm sure it does." She knew it did, actually. At least from her point of view. "But you have a child now, and I have a career that's very important to me."

"Is it because of Brielle? You don't date men with kids...?"

Part of why she gravitated toward older men was because she didn't have to worry about them having little children— or wanting any. But that wasn't the reason for her decision about Reed.

"My decision is based on our past experience together."

He leaned closer. "I thought we could explore being together—see if that trip was a fluke or not."

Anika stepped back. His nearness made her jittery. Actions speak louder than words, the saying went. She'd observed his actions and believed he cared. Then his words had cut her in two.

"To what end?"

"Anika—"

"You hurt me, Reed. Yes, I know we spent less than a week together, but you hurt me. You helped me get over my boyfriend and heal from his rejection, then you twisted the knife in me again." Anika took a deep breath. She was getting emotional.

"You never told me why the two of you broke up."

"The reason doesn't matter." She clasped her shaking hands together. "Bottom line, I don't trust you, and I'm not convinced you're not the same kind of man simply because you say so."

"I am different. And what I feel for you is real."

"What you feel for me? After all this time, what do you think that is? Lust?"

"Not just lust," he said with a flash of anger. "It wasn't just lust then and it's not simply lust now." His jaw hardened. "I don't know how to explain, but for the past seven years, I've thought about you and wondered where you were and if you were okay. I panicked, because you represented change I wasn't ready to embrace. I can see all of that clearly now, but I couldn't then."

"I'm so happy for you, but that's not my problem. I just want to do my job and move on. Please don't make this difficult for me. If you prefer, I could see if Laura would reassign your project—"

"No!" He looked at her aghast.

"Then you have to respect my request to stop." Her hands fisted at her sides and her voice got louder as desperation sank its savage claws into her. "I don't want to explore a relationship with you."

"Respect your wishes." He laughed softly, bitterly.

"Or I'll ask to have you reassigned."

"You want to get away from me that bad, princess?"

The softly spoken endearment was almost her undoing. He definitely wasn't playing fair. "Only if you persist."

His face cemented into hard lines. "Understood."

Their gazes locked as her heart battered her chest.

"Hello there!" A cheery salutation broke the stare off. It came from a dark-haired woman who'd walked up carrying a toddler in her arms. A little girl who appeared to be about five years old rode ahead on a scooter with a helmet on.

"Hi, Dharma." Reed didn't bother summoning a smile for his neighbor.

She was all smiles, however. "Hello, Reed." Her eyes swept his tall frame, full of feminine appreciation.

Reed introduced both women.

"An interior designer. How fascinating. Making some changes to the house?"

"A few things," Reed muttered. Clearly uninterested in the conversation, he kept his attention on Anika.

"I can't use your services right now, but I'm sure one of my friends could at some point. Nothing too drastic, you understand. The women I'm thinking about are in the same boat as me—*divorced*, single moms who don't have a spare nickel." Dharma laughed, slanting a glance at Reed to gauge his reaction. He ignored her. "Do you have any cards with you?" she asked.

"I do." Anika retrieved three from her purse. "Here you go." She handed them over.

"Thank you so much. I'm sure I'll be sending business your way in the near future." She hoisted her son higher on her hip. "Reed, I hope we'll see you at the neighborhood Easter party. It's a lot of fun, and I'm sure Brielle will enjoy it. The kids have a blast hunting for the eggs. And we still have to set up a play date for our girls."

"I'll work on that."

"Anika, it was nice to meet you." She walked away, calling out to her daughter, "Honey, slow down. Don't get too far ahead of me."

"There's the relationship you should explore," Anika said.

"I'm not interested in her."

"And I'm not interested in you."

Quiet.

"Funny. I don't believe that."

"I see you still have a big ego."

"It's not ego. It's the truth."

"I don't want to talk about this anymore."

"Why not?"

"Why not?" She let out a humorless laugh. "What do you want to talk about? You left."

"I didn't want to."

"If you didn't want to, then why did you?" She only gave him a second to respond before she launched into her own explanation. "You left because you wanted to. I was just another notch on your belt."

"That's not true."

"Yes, it is. Let's not make what happened into more than it was. We had fun. Isn't that what you said? It's over. It's done. Two young people happened to be in Venice at the same time and hooked up. It's one of those stories you tell about your wild younger days, but it's just a story. So do me a favor, Reed. Stop talking about it. I did what you asked. I forgot about you."

Dark color blazed across his cheekbones. "Fine. I'll respect your wishes—for now."

It was unnerving how direct he was about his intentions. He headed back up the walkway.

Anika took two steps after him. "What did you mean by that?"

"Can't wait to see those designs. Bye, Anika."

"Reed, what did you mean by that?"

He stopped at the stairs leading up to the porch. "Don't go getting any ideas and asking your boss to get reassigned. I'd hate to share with Judge Evers that my experience with your design firm didn't go as well as she thought it would. It might mean you don't get any more referrals." He paused long enough to let the words sink in. "Have a good afternoon." He disappeared inside the house.

Anika stood there for a few minutes longer, her mouth hanging open in shock. He'd threatened her to ensure they continued working together. The gall. The audacity!

She marched around to the driver's side and hopped into her car. Gripping the steering wheel and silently fuming, she drove away from the neighborhood, fast. So she could escape this new determined Reed, and the memories of their time together.

CHAPTER 6

Venice

    *T*hey took the *vaporetto*, or waterbus, to Murano. Murano was a quieter, calmer part of Venice. Though technically a series of islands linked together by bridges, Murano was known as the Glass Island. Anika was excited to see the glassblowers in action. She'd read up on the practice of glassmaking the night before and learned that because of the fire hazard it presented, in 1291 the Venetian Republic ordered glassmakers to move their foundries to Murano. Not long after, the artisans became leaders in the community, their social status elevated to the point that their daughters could marry into blue-blood families.

They visited two museums, the first housed in a former patrician palace where the exhibits delved into the history of making glass, all the way back to Egyptian times. Hours later, Anika was lost in the displays of the second museum, when Reed said, "Okay, time to go."

She looked up from examining a series of colorful glass jars on a raised platform. "What? Why?"

Reed took her hand and pulled her from the room.

"Excuse you. What are you doing?" Anika whispered fiercely, half-jogging to keep up with his long strides. People stared as they hustled by.

"I'm falling asleep. Time for us to check out the real action and watch these guys work."

Outside, he continued to hold her hand under the guise of hurrying her along. She couldn't read anything from his expression. Her insides, however, were going topsy-turvy.

They'd spent almost every waking moment in each other's company during the past two days. Last night they danced the night away—grinding on each other at a nightclub before stumbling back to the hotel, drunk off the energy of partying with other twenty-something-year-olds and tossing back drinks for hours. Anika had never been drunk before and woke up in the middle of the night to throw up. Reed, sensitive guy that he was, refused to let her stay in this morning to nurse her hangover and wallow in self-pity. He gave her a couple aspirins, told her to stay hydrated, and dragged her out on this excursion.

Anika had no doubt Reed was interested in her, but to what extent? Was spending hours upon hours together just a way for him to kill time on the trip? Or did he experience the same tingling sensation in the bottom of his belly the way she did when he touched her—the way he was touching her now? Did his heart fly high in his chest when she approached, the way hers did when she met him each morning for breakfast before they set out to sightsee?

Not wanting to spoil the moment, Anika simply kept her hand ensconced in Reed's, savoring their stroll along the canal walk. Unfortunately, when they arrived at the factory, he released her so she could enter ahead of him. She rubbed her hands together and found a spot near the front where she could see the artisan at work. Reed stood behind her, not touching, but close enough that the heat from his body warmed her back.

When the demonstration began, the speaker described the process in accented English, while the artisan worked the glass with care and precision. In less than ten minutes he'd turned a shapeless piece of silica into a sparkling blue and white vase by alternating between softening it with heat in a giant oven and shaping it with heavy steel tools.

Afterward, everyone filed into the adjacent shop, a bright colorful contrast to the dark gray of the workshop. White walls presented the perfect backdrop where paperweights, jewelry, and other knickknacks filled the counters and shelves.

"What did you think?" Anika asked.

"Not bad. Good choice."

She scanned a table with glass jewelry and beads and picked up a necklace with green, gold, and red geometric shapes on gold-plated wire, turning it over in her hand. "I should get a gift for my mom. She loves jewelry like I do."

"Get it."

"Can't. I'm on a budget. I shouldn't even be looking."

"I'm on a budget, too, but if I see something I really want, I get it. Life's short. You never know when you'll get sick or, basically, when your last day is."

"Sheesh. That's a depressing thing to say."

"It's reality."

Anika picked up a small bauble among a group of items in the shape of candies. "Did someone close to you die recently?"

"Not recently. My mom."

She glanced up, her heart going out to him. "I'm sorry."

He shrugged. "Happens."

He sounded flippant, but she sensed the change in him.

"When?"

"Junior high. This is pretty. What do you think?" He showed her a necklace with a gold and red heart pendant and six matching red and gold beads on the eighteen-inch chain. He obviously didn't want to talk about his mother.

"It's gorgeous, but I couldn't afford it."

"Fine, I'll get it for you."

"What? I can't let you do that."

"I'm doing it anyway. Nothing you can do about it." He grinned his lazy smile and marched over to one of the sales clerks with the necklace in hand.

Anika rushed after him. "Reed, stop, really."

"I'll take this," he said, completely ignoring her.

The woman smiled and rang up the sale while Anika hung back, unsure of what to do or say. She loved the necklace but didn't think Reed should buy it for her.

"Here you go. Your necklace and a certificate of authenticity from the factory." Reed handed her a little bag with the boxed jewelry.

"I don't know what to say."

"Just say thanks."

"Thanks," Anika said quietly.

"Come on, I'm starving. Let's see if we can find something to eat at one of the cafes."

They walked out of the store and into the street.

"Why'd you do that?" Anika asked after they'd been walking for a while.

"Because I wanted to."

"But why?"

He stopped and shoved his hands in his pockets. "My mother is dead." His eyes clouded with grief and loss. "The reason I included Venice on my trip is because she always talked about this place. She wanted to see it, even had the Grand Canal as a screensaver on her computer. 'One day, Reed. One day we're gonna go there.'" He paused, swallowing hard. "She ate right—cutting out sugar and gluten and all that stuff. She worked hard and saved money *for the future*, she always said. She did everything right, you know?

48

But that didn't stop death from coming for her before she turned forty and realized her plans. I don't want to be like that. I'm living my life. I'm eating the burger and having dessert afterward."

He smiled. "Might as well enjoy myself. Maybe I'm just enjoying myself for her, you know? If she were here and wanted that necklace, I would have gotten for her, because she'd never get it for herself. It's just a necklace, Anika. It won't break me, and I want you to have it."

"Thank you," she said quietly. Her hand tightened around the box. "Where are you headed after Venice?"

"Up to Turin and then France. Then I'm going to Spain, Portugal, and ending my trip in England before heading home. How about you? What are you going to do?"

Anika shrugged. "Go home and try to find a job."

His eyes narrowed. "What about Emerson?"

"The truth?"

"Of course."

She laughed softly. "He and I broke up."

"No way."

She nodded, her face heating in embarrassment. "He broke up with me, and that's why I'm here alone." An eternal optimist, she still believed in romance and trusted that one day she'd meet someone who would appreciate her.

"Yeah, well, he was a jerk. He didn't deserve you. You could do better."

Anika watched him, askance. In all honesty, she should have seen through Emerson. She'd been so in love with the idea of love, she'd ignored the signs indicative of his true character. "Did you know him well?"

"No, but I could tell he was a jerk. He had that jerk walk and he was a dick in intramural sports. You were too good for him."

"Now you're making me blush."

"It's the truth. I can't think of a single good reason why he would break up with you."

Anika lowered her gaze. "He had his reasons."

"Well, I guess we both got dumped."

"Who dumped you?"

"Deanna."

"The girl on the softball team?"

"Yep," he replied, nodding.

"You don't seem too broken up about it."

"I'm not. She did me a favor." He resumed walking and Anika followed.

"So what do you think is wrong with us?" she asked.

"Who says it's us? Maybe it's them."

"You're so sure?"

"Absolutely."

He lifted his head at a cocky angle. Anika wished she had his confidence.

"Maybe in your case, but not mine."

You're broken. She couldn't get Emerson's ugly words out of her head. He'd said them after she told him she couldn't have kids. At eighteen she'd had her ovaries removed because of painful cysts. She'd opted for hormone therapy, suffering through breast tenderness and vaginal bleeding for weeks that made her think she should have waited and sought out a different solution. The symptoms subsided after a month, but the regret and sense of loss persisted. There were no Mother's Day celebrations in her future, and Emerson revived her anguish with his brutal words.

Reed stopped her with a hand on her arm. "Hey, whatever he said, he's wrong. There's nothing wrong with you. You're pretty and smart and really nice. It's his loss."

"Pretty and smart and nice?" She latched on to the words.

His eyes narrowed. "Don't let the compliments go to your head."

She laughed.

Reed didn't laugh, though. "Seriously. There's nothing wrong with you."

He sounded so sincere that she believed him.

She hadn't thought about Emerson in over twenty-four hours, and even now he was a fleeting thought, a cloudy memory when compared the vivid imagery of Reed before her. A few days in his company and she was developing feelings for him, knowing full well it was a bad idea.

Perhaps because she was particularly vulnerable since the abrupt end to her last relationship, but she wondered what it would be like to be his girlfriend. Getting involved with him was a non-starter—a rebound thing that she knew she'd end up regretting. She wasn't here to get her emotions tangled up in another man—no matter how attractive, funny, and charming.

So a fling, perhaps? On another continent, did it even count? She saw Reed with new eyes.

"Thanks. I needed to hear all of that."

The lazy smile came back, and the measured way he looked at her suggested he was reassessing her, too. "I meant every word. All of that."

CHAPTER 7

*P*at, *pat*, *pat*.

    Reed awoke to three gentle slaps to the face.

"Daddy."

He cracked his eyes. Brielle stood at the side of the bed, her face so close to his, her breath touched his nose. She was clutching Mr. Elephant—one of three companions she alternated between each night.

"Are you awake?" she whispered, making direct eye contact. Maybe he should get her eyes checked.

"I am now," Reed muttered.

"I think there's a monster in my room."

"Honey, we've been through this. There's no such thing as monsters."

"B-but I heard something, Daddy." No way he could resist the gentle whine of her voice.

Online research confirmed he was doing all the right things on the monster front—acknowledging her fear, telling the truth that monsters didn't exist, and establishing trust by showing her there was nothing in the closet or under the bed. He hoped she'd soon grow accustomed to the house and wouldn't wake up in the middle of the night anymore, fearful of the unknown.

Reed swung his feet over the side of the bed and sat there for a minute, rubbing sleep from his eyes with the heels of his palms. Damn, he was tired. Tax season would be over soon, but his schedule was packed and stressful until mid-April.

Reed removed the flashlight from the drawer of his night-stand. "All right baby, let's go check the room." He took her hand and they walked down the hall.

A battery-powered mermaid nightlight rested on the round white table next to Brielle's bed. It gave off a rose-hued glow, but alternated to purple, blue, and other colors during the night.

"Where'd you hear the monster?" Reed asked.

"In there." Brielle pointed at the closet.

Reed flicked on the flashlight and swung open the door. Only shoes and clothes were inside. He made sure to turn the light into every corner so Brielle, who peered from behind his leg, could clearly see.

"I don't see anything. Do you?" he asked.

"No."

He closed the door and then crouched before the bed. Lifting the skirt, he waved the flashlight under it. Brielle laid down on the floor beside him, watching the light flicker over the carpet.

"I don't see anything? Do you?" Reed asked.

"No."

They both stood and he set the flashlight on the table by her bed.

"I thought I heard something. I'm not a liar," Brielle said, her voice sounding wobbly. Reed knew she felt guilty for waking him up.

He lowered to his haunches. "I believe you, sweetheart, but there's nothing there. We checked together. I checked and you checked with me, right?" She nodded. "Okay, let's get you in bed now. It's late."

He pulled back the sheets and helped her into the bed.

"Remember, there are no monsters. They're only pretend on TV and in books."

"I know, Daddy."

Now she sounded impatient. Reed smiled slightly.

Carefully tucking her in, he asked, "Are you comfy?"

"Um, I think I don't want Mr. Elephant tonight. Can I have Baby Giraffe? He wants me to hold him."

"That's right, I heard him say so."

"He can't talk, Daddy." She laughed, as if he'd said the silliest thing she'd ever heard.

Right. He needed to remember that Baby Giraffe could convey the need to be held without talking.

Reed took the stuffed elephant, placed it next to Teddy on the lid of her box of toys, and brought back Baby Giraffe. "There you go."

She clutched the animal by its long neck.

"You good now?"

"Yes."

"Did you say your prayers for Mommy tonight?"

"Yes. And you and Grandma and Grandpa and Pop Pop."

"Good girl." Reed kissed her forehead. "Good night."

Because she expected him to stay, he sat on the floor beside the bed and rested his back against the wall. Across the room, a narrow bookcase with picture books and a shelf dedicated to photos of Brielle and her mother, Layla, sat in a corner. Brielle's grandmother, Nanette, had recently sent the collection and he put them on display. The one to the front was a black and white photo of Layla and Brielle at two. In the close-up they had their cheeks pressed together, laughing into the camera. It was his favorite.

Of course thinking about Layla made him think about Anika. Almost every woman he'd been involved with since

Anika had been black, as if he'd tried to recreate the same passion and intensity they'd shared. Yet none of them had been right. None of those relationships lasted. Picking women of the same race or appearance couldn't duplicate what they'd had. What made him and Anika work was her personality. And none of those women were her, the person she was inside.

He sat there until Brielle's even breathing became audible, but instead of going back to his room, he eased onto her twin bed. His feet hung off the side, but he simply wanted to be close to her for a bit.

He still harbored guilt about her mother. He should have married Layla and given her the life she obviously wanted but he pretended to believe she didn't need. Because he suspected, despite her comments to the contrary, if he'd asked her to marry him—put in a serious effort—she would have said yes.

Reed closed his eyes. He was pretty sure God had a sense of humor. After all the shit he'd done, God saw fit to give him a daughter. Before Brielle's mother passed away, he'd been a part-time dad. Not even part-time, with him living in New York and Layla living in Texas. Now that he filled both parental roles, he doubted his ability to master his responsibilities as protector, nurturer, teacher. How the heck did other single parents do it? Even with help, taking care of Brielle was a lot of work.

Most of all, removing her from what was familiar in Dallas filled him with guilt. Her grandparents, who'd helped raise her, aunts, uncles, and cousins all lived in the area and she'd grown up around them. They hadn't been pleased when he'd come to take her but respected his rights as her father.

Brielle moaned in her sleep and rolled onto her back, one arm still locked around Baby Giraffe, the other sprawled out to her side. Her eyelids twitched and then stopped. Her rough breathing resumed its even tempo.

He watched her sleep, pride filling his chest. She'd changed him from a selfish bachelor into a responsible adult. She was the one thing he'd done right. How lucky was he to be the father of this kid? Even when she drove him nuts with *Why* questions every five seconds.

Daddy, why do I have to take a bath every night? I hate baths.

Because if you don't, you'll stink.

Why?

Because all the sweat and dirt that accumulated throughout the day will stay on your skin and make you smell bad.

Why?

Because it does, and you have to wash it off.

Why?

Because I said so.

Reed laughed softly and sat up.

He still had to figure out how to handle her tantrums. It was important for Brielle to maintain a relationship with her grandmother, but he dreaded the end of those phone calls. They missed her, and it was obvious she missed them, too. Each time his daughter hung up, she fell into a sullen mood. Then, her attitude morphed into cranky and difficult tantrums.

Had he made a mistake bringing her to Atlanta? He hated seeing his little girl go through any kind of emotional turmoil and wasn't one hundred percent certain he'd done the right thing.

"Give her time," his cousin's wife had said.

He was trying, but it was hard.

"Do what's best for my grandbaby. Bring her back," Brielle's grandmother had said when he spoke to her last.

Maybe he would eventually have to take her back, but not now. He still had time.

He wasn't ready to give up yet.

CHAPTER 8

*T*oday was demolition day.

Anika strolled past the two trucks parked in Reed's driveway. Reed had liked her idea of opening up the kitchen to the den, so Edgar and his crew were going to knock down the partial wall between both rooms.

Anika rang the doorbell.

She had a full day planned. A stop at another house going through demolition across town, with much more work to be done. She also had to make a trip to the building surplus warehouse, the lumber yard, and pay a visit to a craftsman to inspect a custom cabinet he was building for a client. To accommodate the day, she'd dressed comfortably in jeans, Keds, and a fitted orange T-shirt.

The high-pitched scream of a child came from the other side of the door, and Anika took an involuntary step back.

Another scream came loud and clear, and in the next instant, the door swung open. Reed stood shirtless before her, holding a wriggling Brielle wearing only a pair of striped panties, and whose uncombed curly hair resembled a multitude of wires all over her head.

Anika's gaze shifted from the red-faced little girl to the

tight-lipped grimace of her father. And then her gaze went lower. To the short, silky hairs on his chest that angled down into the low-slung jeans on his hips. Half-dressed and with fine bristles covering his jaw and chin, Reed looked exhausted but sexy.

Anika's mouth went dry, and she forced her gaze to return to his face. "I came to check on the work," she half yelled over the screaming child. Brielle flung her body backward in Reed's arms and screamed even louder, tears pouring down her cheeks. Anika winced, shoulders lifting toward her ears at the eardrum-splitting cry. With those lungs, Brielle had a future in the opera.

Poor Reed appeared to be at the end of his rope, his hair uncombed and frustration evident in his eyes right before he closed them and took a deep breath.

"I'm sorry about this. The workers are already here. Come on in." He moved aside so Anika could enter and shut the door. "If you don't mind, could you—" He broke off as the little soprano lurched backward again. "Brielle, behave yourself," he muttered through clenched teeth.

The chastisement didn't do anything to stop the screaming and only made Brielle add kicking to the tantrum.

"What's wrong with her?" Anika hollered to be heard above the noise.

"She's just—"

Brielle jerked again, this time lunging toward Anika. The sudden movement made Anika lift her hands, but Reed caught the girl.

"I'm sorry." He gritted his teeth, struggling to maintain a hold on Brielle, who wriggled her tiny body with the speed and dexterity of a serpent. "I'll get her upstairs and try to calm her down."

"No! No!" Brielle screamed at the top of her lungs. Reaching for Anika.

"I'll only be a minute," Reed said, an apologetic expression on his face. He turned toward the staircase and Brielle screamed and continued to reach for Anika.

He was a quarter of the way up the staircase when Anika called out, "I can hold her." Why had she said that?

Reed managed a precarious balancing act on the stairs with his wiggling daughter. "What?"

"I—I can hold her. If it'll help."

He hesitated, taking stock of Brielle's mottled, tear-streaked face. "I don't think that's a good idea. She's a handful."

"I have nieces and nephews," Anika assured him, feeling more confident.

Clearly still doubtful, Reed slowly descended the stairs and after a few seconds of hesitation, handed over Brielle.

Anika gathered the upset child to her chest. "What's wrong, sweetie? Hmm?"

She spoke in a quiet, soothing voice and rocked Brielle in her arms until the screams quieted to a low whine. With the combination of soft tones and the swaying motion, Brielle relaxed. She rested her head on Anika's shoulder and huffed out an exhausted breath.

Reed stared. "How did you do that?"

"Magic," Anika quipped. She rubbed Brielle's back and could feel the little girl's racing heart slowing down to normal.

"Usually I'm more together than this, but man, it's been a morning." Reed ran both hands down his face. "Mrs. Miller is running late and should be here any minute. Thank you."

"No problem." She'd always had a good rapport with children. Her little cousins adored her, her friends' kids always looked forward to her visits, and her brother's little ones showered her with kisses every time they visited. "I think kids like me because I smell like strawberries." She grinned.

Reed let out a tired laugh, and then the amusement slid from his face. "Yeah, you do," he said in a low voice.

The air between them sizzled, and Anika quickly averted her eyes, gently patting Brielle on the back. "I can keep an eye on her while you finish getting dressed." She couldn't handle watching him walk around half-naked. He should put on a shirt right away.

"I couldn't ask you to do that."

"I don't mind."

"Are you sure?"

"Absolutely. Brielle and I are buddies now, and it'll give me time to hang out with my new friend." Anika continued to sway. Brielle's ruddy, tear-stained cheek rested on her shoulder as she breathed evenly through her partially open mouth.

"Well, if you're sure…"

"I don't mind at all."

The front door opened and Mrs. Miller walked in. Her eyes widened as she quickly assessed the situation. "Another tantrum?" Sympathy filled her eyes.

"Yes," Reed replied.

"She got another phone call?"

Reed swallowed. "Yeah."

"Phone call?" Anika asked.

"Long story," Reed replied. "Mrs. Miller can take over now, and you can check on the progress of the work."

"Oh. Of course." Reluctantly, Anika gave up Brielle to her nanny. The loss of weight left a void in her arms and chest. She'd become much too comfortable holding the little girl in her arms. She swallowed back a pained whimper that threatened to come out.

"Have you had breakfast?" Mrs. Miller cradled Brielle against her bosom. Her gaze encompassed Reed and Anika.

"I have another appointment after this, so I won't be able to stay," Anika replied. "Thank you."

"I'm fine. I'll grab an apple," Reed said.

"All right then." Mrs. Miller climbed the stairs with Brielle in her arms.

"If you don't mind, I'll take you up on that offer to finish getting dressed. Give me five minutes and I'll be right back."

"Take your time." Anika watched him ascend the stairs, eyes lingering on his body. It was difficult not to stare at his firm bottom, lean hips, and broad, tanned back rippling with muscles. She was very familiar with the silky but firm texture of those muscles. She'd caressed them in adoration and gripped them in the throes of ecstasy.

Anika swallowed hard and shook her head before going in search of the workers. They were in the process of covering the floors with a temporary covering and a plastic tarp to protect from debris and dust.

She chatted with the men until Reed returned, much more relaxed with his hair combed and a gray T-shirt with *Accountants do it better on the front*. She looked away from the words and tried not to think about what they meant.

A frown of worry descended on Reed's features.

Anika placed her hands on her hips. "You're not getting cold feet are you?"

"What would happen if I did?" His eyes traveled over the men moving around the room.

"I'm going to tell you what I tell all of our clients," Edgar said, a tall, lanky Black man with a kind face and a good sense of humor. "Don't freak out when you see the carnage."

"There's going to be carnage?" Now Reed appeared really perturbed.

Anika covered her mouth to keep from busting out laughing. "Believe me, you're going to be very happy with the final result. As a matter of fact, we want you to get involved in the process."

"What do you want me to do?" Reed asked, in a slow, suspicious voice.

Edgar held up a pair of safety goggles, gloves, and a sledgehammer. "You're going to get us started." He handed Reed the tools.

Reed studied the items for a few seconds. "I'll do this on one condition."

"What's that?"

"That Anika does it with me. Do you have another set of goggles and a hammer?"

"Sure do."

Edgar handed the same items to Anika, and she groaned. "Great."

Within minutes, she and Reed were wearing the protective gear and she positioned herself with her feet shoulder-width apart in front of the wall.

"For your information, I've done this before," she told Reed.

She'd aided on occasion in the knocking down of a wall, but this process was for the clients, to give them a sense of participation and also a way to expel any pent-up tension they held in about the demolition. The true work would be done by the men with power tools, much faster and with greater efficiency.

"I can't imagine that you could've ever gotten your hands dirty," Reed said.

Edgar averted his face in a vain attempt to hide his laughter, and stepped out of the way.

Anika shot them both dirty looks. "Ha. Ha. Watch my dust."

"All right, let's do this!" Edgar said.

She and Reed swung hard, landing deep gashing holes into the drywall. Over and over, they pummeled the wall with the sledgehammers, breaking off huge chunks that crashed to the floor. After a few minutes they had expended quite a bit of energy, and beads of perspiration dotted Anika's forehead.

"Damn, this is hard work," Reed finally said.

Breathing heavily, Anika laughed. "It's a good way to get your exercise."

"All right you two, I'll take those," Edgar said.

They handed him the tools and removed the gear. Anika wiped her damp forehead with the back of her hand. "I'll let you guys finish up, but I gave you a good start."

"What would we do without you?" Edgar blew her a kiss and she blew one back.

She and Reed walked to the front of the house so Edgar and the men could seal off the room and get down to the real work.

They strolled down the walkway to her car. "You running off already?" Reed asked.

Anika nodded. "I'm going to check on another demolition. Edgar's really good at his job, so I have no concerns."

Reed nodded his understanding. Compared to only a few minutes ago when he'd attacked the wall with her, his demeanor had become significantly more reserved.

"I appreciate your help with Brielle."

Anika stopped at her vehicle and stuffed her hands into the back pocket of her jeans. "What caused such a meltdown?"

"She talked to her grandmother, Nanette, yesterday." He ran a weary hand through his hair. "She misses her, or Nanette reminds her of missing her mother. Or some combination." He expelled a heavy breath. "Anyway, when she gets like that, she doesn't want anything to do with me. I thought only Mrs. Miller could calm her, but maybe she prefers a woman's touch during those moments."

"I'm glad I could help."

"I'll have to find a way to thank you."

"No need."

"I'll be the judge of that."

"So you're just going to force something on me?" she laughed nervously.

"I did it before." The corner of his mouth lifted into a sexy smile, and Anika's stomach contracted. He was referring to the glass necklace he'd bought for her on Murano. "Do you still have it—the necklace?"

The weight of the moment sat on the air like heavy fog.

"Yes." She wished she had a different answer, but it sat in her jewelry box, a constant reminder of what could have been. A reminder that she'd belonged to him and she'd never recovered.

"I thought for sure you'd toss it."

"It's too pretty to toss."

"Is that the only reason?"

Anika kicked at a pebble, refusing to answer.

"Thanks."

She looked up. "For what?" She couldn't decipher the look in his eyes.

"For giving me hope."

She stepped back. She didn't want to offer hope or feel it. Hope meant expectations that could end in painful disappointment. Hope was the enemy.

"I'd better go."

Anika twisted away with an abrupt turn and didn't wait for Reed to acknowledge her departure. She hopped in her car, slammed the door, and drove away. In the rearview mirror, Reed stood in the street, thumbs hooked in the loops of his jeans, staring after her.

She blinked back tears and pounded her palm against the steering wheel. "Shit, shit, shit."

In mere weeks, her life had gone from stable to unstable. Reed awakened a hunger in her that she struggled to contain, knowing full well that if she continued to spend time with him, the hunger would definitely consume her.

CHAPTER 9

*T*he house was quiet.

Reed turned out the kitchen light but paused for a moment to survey the work that had already been completed. Anika had been right. The new open floor plan was much better than what he had before, and allowed more light into both the kitchen and the den.

The painters had arrived today and the house smelled like...well, it smelled like paint. Brielle complained, but he assured her the odor wouldn't last.

He climbed the stairs and stopped at his daughter's bedroom door. Cracking it open, he peeked in. The mermaid light sprayed purple color against the wall and Brielle slept peacefully, tonight holding Teddy in the customary chokehold.

He went down the hall to his office and kept the door open so he could hear if she woke up. Anika had recommended some other colors to lighten up the dark décor of chocolate walls, chocolate built-in shelves, and a chocolate desk—incorporating tan chairs, a new light fixture, and Roman shades. He'd requested she not wait to have the items delivered, and their presence gave the room a lighter feel but maintained the cozy atmosphere he needed to concentrate.

Reed logged into the system at work, but as he did so, a thought came to him. He hadn't talked to Anika since Friday when she helped him with Brielle. He wanted to hear her voice, but not to discuss furniture patterns or color swatches.

He needed to properly thank her, as promised. Although he admitted to himself that calling to thank Anika was an excuse, he picked up the phone anyway.

He'd been wound up the past couple of days at work and had remained in his office to keep from snapping at staff. Brielle tended to be rather cautious around strangers, but she'd taken to Anika right away, and seeing Anika with his daughter—the way she'd handled her with gentleness and care, and the way Brielle had taken to her—had done something to him. It planted a seed that sprouted a litany of ideas he couldn't shake.

Anika answered on the first ring. "Hello?"

He held his breath for a second. He couldn't control the automatic way his body reacted to her every single time. There was a loosening in his chest, as if his heart had unfurled from a tight knot.

"I hope I didn't call you too late."

"Not at all. I'm working on an idea for Brielle's room, and I'll have something to share with you soon. There's just one piece of information that I'm waiting on. What can I do for you?"

So polite. So professional. When what he wanted from her was anything but politeness and professionalism.

"Actually, it's what I can do for you."

Pause. "Oh?"

He imagined a curious expression on her face. "Don't sound so worried. I just want to thank you for helping me with Brielle last week. When she throws a tantrum, it can be overwhelming." He walked over to the window overlooking the front yard. From here he had a good view of the neighborhood. The family across the street had smoke winding up the back of their house. Probably cooking out again. They did that all hours of the day or night.

"I'm fairly certain you're not the only parent who feels overwhelmed at times. You're doing the best you can, and you love your daughter. That's half of what being a good parent is all about."

"What do you think the other half is?"

"Keeping an eye on them so they don't burn the house down," Anika quipped.

He smiled, leaning a shoulder against the window. "Are you talking from experience? Were *you* that kid?"

"I plead the fifth." Anika giggled. Man, he loved the sound of her joy. "Was there something else?" He heard her moving around.

"Actually, there is." He'd gone from wanting to hear her voice to desperately needing to see her. "I'd like to take you to dinner and show you how much I appreciate your help."

She stopped moving. "Dinner?"

"Yeah, dinner. You know, that meal you eat at the end of the day, often between six and eight." He kept his voice light even as tension permeated every cell of his body.

"I know what dinner is, smarty pants." Pause again, this time longer. "You don't have to do that."

"I want to, and I'm not taking no for an answer."

"So if I decline, you're going to do, what exactly?"

"Drive over to your office and kidnap you."

She laughed. "Oh really? You really want to show your appreciation, huh?"

"I really do." His appreciation was sincere, but certainly not his sole motivation to see her. "So what do you say? Can I get a yes? Or do you have plans this weekend?"

He couldn't hear anything on the opposite end of the line and waited in the tense silence, fully prepared to argue her down or suggest another night if she declined his invitation.

"I don't have plans this weekend, but you don't have to take me out. I didn't mind helping."

"I want to do it anyway. It's the least I could do for saving my sanity, and last I checked, calming angry, crying four-year-olds is not in the job description of an interior designer."

"You have a point." She heard the smile in his voice. "Okay, you've talked me into it."

He didn't realize how much nervous tension had taken over his body until she readily agreed. His body sagged, his head bowing in relief. "How about Saturday night?" He had to work late on Friday night but only half day on Saturday.

"Saturday works."

"Which restaurant?"

"How about Paschal's Restaurant?"

"Sounds vaguely familiar, but it's up to you. As long as the food is good, I'm open."

"Believe me, it's good."

"It's a date, then."

Slight pause. "Yes, it's a date. I'll meet you there."

"See you then."

After they hung up, Reed remained at the window, staring out at the dark surroundings, one hand stuffed into his pocket. He wondered if he was pushing too hard but couldn't stop himself. He was more convinced than ever that Anika was the one person missing from his life. Seven years ago he'd fought against such a sobering belief, convinced that such a short period of time was surely not enough to establish a genuine connection.

But that summer, playful banter had turned into light flirtation. Light flirtation had turned into simmering need. Then one night it blossomed into more. Out of control. Plenty of heat. Plenty of passion.

Once should have been enough, but it wasn't.
He'd spent the night in her bed. In her room. In her.

CHAPTER 10

Venice

*A*nika closed her eyes and sighed, her lashes brushing against her cheeks. "I'm having such a good time."

They were standing in the hallway outside her door after another fun-filled day. She had talked him into visiting Aman Canal Grande Venice Resort, a sixteenth century building where Amal and George Clooney were married. They took a lot of photos. In his opinion, too many, but he went along with whatever she suggested because her excitement was contagious.

He could well imagine his mother enjoying herself just as much. A cluster of regret ballooned in his chest. Once again, he wished she'd had the chance to visit before she died.

After the resort, he and Anika sat at a waterside cafe, listening to the sea slosh against the sides of the boats docked nearby and tossing back bottles of Orangina soda. They'd ended the day with an evening gondola ride. Their gondolier had gone all out, wearing the straw hat with a red ribbon around it and singing at the top of his lungs in a perfect tenor as they coasted down the canals with the setting sun as a backdrop.

They'd shared the boat with another couple, but Reed had only paid attention to Anika. He'd only listened to her voice and watched her reaction to everything they saw. The way she laughed when the gondolier made a joke or paid avid attention to his history lesson about the city and the canals. She took photos of the Rialto bridge, one of four bridges that spanned the Grand Canal and the oldest of the lot, and waved to passengers in other gondolas.

He was more than simply attracted to her. He could admit that now. He'd been attracted to plenty of women before, but this was deeper and almost tangible. It was more personal—more intimate. Being with Anika made everything better. The wine sweeter. The sun brighter.

Her subtle sexuality was completely addictive, manifesting into a sensation that gripped him by the chest and refused to let go. She helped him forget the uncertainty of his future and every minute they spent apart, he longed for the next time he'd see her. Their constant interaction was not enough, and he worried about this growing attachment to her when he'd never needed anyone before.

Reed's jaw tightened, and when she opened her eyes, he barely resisted the urge to drag her into his arms and kiss her. All day he'd pondered the taste of her lips.

"Glad you enjoyed yourself," he said.

She eyed him, as if trying to figure out what he was thinking. She didn't want to know.

"I guess I better go to bed. I'll see you in the morning," Anika said quietly.

She smiled a little smile, the same one he often caught on her face. It filtered into her eyes the way sunlight broke through the clouds and illuminated the early morning sky.

"Bright and early for breakfast," he said, not moving.

Neither budged from their positions, and that's when he

knew, if he made a move right now, she would let him not only kiss her, she would let him make love to her. They were in Italy, after all. And they'd just taken a gondola ride in one of the most romantic cities in the world. But he didn't want to start something he couldn't finish, and she struck him as a forever kind of woman.

Reed swallowed. "Go inside, Anika." Being a gentleman sucked.

Hurt filled her eyes, but she straightened her back. "What if I don't want to," she whispered.

An unusual tightening caught hold of his gut. "Then I won't be responsible for what happens."

"I'm willing to take that chance."

A decent man would recognize her vulnerability and walk away; and he wanted to, except no one had ever accused him of being decent. He couldn't imagine leaving when he'd thought of little else but sleeping with her for the past few days. Sweet, sweet Anika. That's what he thought of her. In her pastel colors and sleek ponytails.

What would she look like naked, her golden brown body bared in its entirety for his hungry gaze? With her long hair mussed and spilling across her shoulders in unruly disarray? With her lips swollen from his kisses even as they offered him more sensual bliss?

"You sure about that?" Reed asked. Crushing tension built in his groin.

"Yes." Three letters, and among the most powerful words in the English language. Three letters that took him one step closer to the fantasy that plagued his thoughts and tortured his body at night.

Without hesitation, Reed bent his head and slanted his mouth over hers. She didn't flinch or pull back, but the initial introduction of their lips to each other was an awkward and tentative act. Once he relaxed into it, white hot heat spiraled through his veins. The next thing he knew, he had her pushed up against the wall, the brutal pounding of his heart ramming against his rib cage. Cupping the back of her head with one hand, he devoured her mouth, kissing her with demand. Kissing her with the certainty of how the night would end.

A soft mewl echoed in the back of her throat as she drew him closer by fisting a hand in his shirt. He ran his hands under her skirt, bunching the material around her upper thighs. Dragging her hips into his, he gripped her tight little ass, and when she made the same sound again, Reed knew there was no turning back.

"Key," he ground out.

Anika fumbled in her purse for the card and then turned toward the door. Reed took the opportunity to grab her by the hips and press his hard erection against the pliable cushion of her bottom. With his lips on the side of her neck, she let them into the room.

He took charge immediately and filled his hands with her breasts, all the while savoring her flavor and the pillowy softness of her lips. They were as succulent and sweet as two ripe plums, and he couldn't get enough as he backed her toward the bed. His mouth returned to the side of her throat, and on a breathy moan, she arched her neck. His tongue slid over the salty skin, and her little sigh encouraged him further.

She started stripping him of his clothes, pulling the shirt over his head and going for the zipper of his jeans with the same enthusiasm with which she'd accepted his kisses. He impatiently helped her with the removal of his pants, tugging them past his hips along with the boxers, and then went to work on her clothes.

He continued to ply her mouth with kisses as his hands busied undressing her. When he'd removed her blouse, he tossed it aside and took in the lovely picture she made—her breasts lush and full, covered in pretty black lace. Off it came, and he hastily he pushed her onto the bed and continued to undress her. She lay there, biting her bottom lip with a mixture of excitement and shyness. His body ached to claim her right away, but he wanted to give her the utmost pleasure.

Within minutes they were both naked and on top of the cool sheets, his hands moving over her soft skin in wonder. Dipping his head, he flicked his tongue over a rosy brown nipple. Breath stuttering, she grabbed a handful of his hair and arched her back. Reed cupped one of her breasts and sucked the pebbled peak into his mouth, listening to her make sounds of pleasure somewhere between a moan and a sigh. So beautiful. So sensual. He felt it all the way down to his groin and was willing to do whatever it took to hear those noises repeatedly throughout the night.

He moved down her sternum toward her belly button, making sure to glide his hands over her skin. She moved restlessly on the bed as he continued his relentless advance even lower.

Reed paused when he saw two faint scars below her belly button, on either side of her abdomen. He touched the one on the right with his forefinger, and she tensed.

"What happened?" he whispered.

"Childhood accident."

"What kind of—"

"I fell on my bike. It was bad. I'd rather not talk about it." Her voice sounded strained. The mood in the room had shifted.

"Hey, I'm sorry." Reed didn't want to spoil the moment, but the thought of her suffering prompted him to press his lips to one scar and then the other—ever so gently to ease her distress.

She relaxed beneath his touch, and he took his time licking every inch of her. She almost jerked off the bed when he claimed the sensitive spot between her legs with his tongue, but he held her down and lapped at the moist flesh, listening to her broken cries of pleasure and choppy pleas for him to stop. Only once he'd had his fill did he continue his descent. He wanted to know all of her, right down to her toes.

Gathering her in his arms, Reed kissed between her breasts.

"Reed," Anika murmured, cradling his face in her hands. She urged him up to her mouth, and they resumed an earth-bending kiss. Skin to skin, their warm bodies became entangled in each other, and Reed slid his hand down her waist and cupped her lush bottom. He squeezed and caressed, grinding his hips into her hers in an erotic simulation of sex.

"Now, sweetheart. I have to have you now." He barely got the words out, panting them against her collarbone.

"Yes, please. I can't wait."

Propelled by the urgency in her voice, Reed retrieved a condom and swiftly came back to the bed. Looking down at her shapely body, his breath caught. Damn, she was incredible.

Bracing on his arms, he fed his body into her glistening sex. He almost lost it right then and had to stop for a moment. One eyelid twitched as he fought to reign himself in. Grinding down on his teeth, he plunged deeper. Anika tossed her head back and lifted into the thrust.

A groan caught in his throat. Goddamn, she was tight. And so wet. The taut clasp of her body felt incredible. *She* was incredible, completely giving herself over to the sensation. Her skin was flushed, eyes half-closed, hands gripping his biceps as she moved in time to his same rhythmic motion.

Her hands shifted all over his skin, his back, his neck, as if she was at a loss to decide where to touch. She pressed her mouth to his jaw and then claimed his lips again, shoving her fingers into his hair, all rough and careless. Her less-than-gentle handling only inflamed his lust. Gritting his teeth, Reed lifted her bottom and angled her hips for a deeper thrust.

The movement made her gasp, inhaling deeply.

"Fucking good, isn't it?" he muttered against her lips. He thrust hard and deep again. This time she cried out louder.

He kept thrusting. She was so warm and slick, he could only keep up that manic motion. Losing himself. Drunk on lust.

Anika gripped his ass, and they moved as if they were made for each other, their lovemaking mixed with heavy pants and frantic kissing.

Until...pulses rocked her body as she came undone, saying his name with an achy cry at the end. Her ragged breathing feathered over the shell of his ear.

Shit.

Reed's control crumbled. He ejaculated so hard and so suddenly, his fingers gripped the pillows on either side of her head as his hips exploded into a frenzy of sporadic pumping. Shuddering as the last bit of cum left his body, he dropped his head into the scented corner of her neck and released a belly-deep groan.

She was perfection. Reed dragged his nose along one soft shoulder, inhaling Anika's delicate floral scent. He sucked on her damp skin—helplessly, tasting more of her even though he should be satisfied.

He rolled onto his side but pulled Anika into his arms so the full length of their bodies meshed together.

"Reed," she said on a sigh. Her eyes were closed and a beatific smile crossed her face.

Gazing at her, Reed finally got the answers to the questions he'd posed to himself earlier. A naked Anika with swollen lips and messy hair was unbelievably sexy.

CHAPTER 11

*S*he was overdressed.

Anika sat in the car, waiting for the valet, staring down at her tan, ankle-length fitted skirt, her right leg peeking through the split on the side. Both arms were bare in the cream one-shoulder top she'd paired with it.

Too late to go home and change now. Besides, she'd tried on three different outfits before settling on this one, rushed out of the house so she wouldn't keep Reed waiting, and still she was running late.

The valet approached and she exited the vehicle and handed over her key.

Paschal's Restaurant was one of her favorite places to eat. Not only did they serve delicious food, but she had fond memories of eating lunch after church with her parents, brothers, and grandmother, discussing the morning's sermon or having spirited but good-natured arguments. And it wasn't unusual for her father, God rest his soul, to strike up a conversation with a nearby table and drag both parties into a political or religious debate.

Anika scanned the restaurant in search of Reed as she

waited her turn behind a small group at the hostess stand. The gentle hum of well-dressed patrons, their quiet discussions and soft laughter filled the room. Male and female servers deftly maneuvered around, carrying trays of colorful drinks and steaming plates of soul food.

After the group before her had been escorted to a table, Anika stepped up. "Hi, I'm meeting someone here." She peered into the dining room. "I don't think he's here yet, but—"

A warm hand settled at the base of her spine, and instinctively, Anika inhaled sharply. The scent of citrus and pine filled her nostrils. She should step away, but the sensation of his touch overtook her entire body, heating her from head to toe and holding her in place.

"Hey, there," Reed said.

He flashed a smile, all charm and sizzle, temporarily rendering Anika unable to speak, unable to breathe, unable to function like a normal human being. As was his habit, he'd forgone a tie, choosing to wear a dark jacket over a crisp white shirt with dark pants.

"You made it," she said.

"Sorry I'm late. Brielle thought it would be funny to hide my shoes. Tickling and threatening didn't work to convince her to tell me where they were."

"What finally worked?"

"Begging."

Anika laughed, albeit shakily, still a bit overwhelmed by his presence. "It's clear who has the control in that house."

"Oh, there's no doubt. And she knows it."

The hostess escorted them to a booth near the back wall. As they sat down, Reed surveyed the loft-style interior, consisting of exposed pipes in the high ceilings, with one wall offering a view of the outdoors through large windows that looked out onto the street. Yellow sconces on the columns projected soft lighting to the interior and cast shadows on the black and white photos of Civil Rights leaders hung on the exposed brick walls.

"I've never eaten here, but I vaguely remember hearing about this restaurant."

"So you don't know its history?" Anika asked.

"No, I don't," Reed admitted.

Excited to share her limited knowledge, Anika set down the menu. "Paschal's was founded in 1947 by brothers Robert and James Paschal. My grandmother told me they started out selling sandwiches and sodas and the business grew into what you see today. They're a black-owned restaurant that was financed by a black-owned bank and insured by a black-owned insurance company. My grandmother said it wasn't unusual to see civil rights leaders eating in the restaurant."

"Like who?"

Anika pointed at the wall above them, where hung a photo of Dr. Martin Luther King, Jr. and one of Joseph E. Lowery receiving the Presidential Medal of Freedom from President Obama. "Dr. King, Representative John Lewis, Ralph David Abernathy, Joseph Lowery—any of them."

"Wow."

Anika nodded. She'd loved hearing the stories her grandmother recounted and was amazed at how African-Americans managed to flourish during times of such adversity. "Rumor has it, Dr. King loved the vegetable soup."

"Have you tried it?"

"Yes, and I agree. It's good."

"What else is good?" Reed skimmed the menu.

"My favorites are the catfish and fried chicken. And you can't go wrong with the macaroni and cheese—oh, and the collard greens. Or the yams. Any of the dishes." Her mouth watered thinking about the choices.

Reed laughed and set down his menu. "How about I order

the fried chicken, mac and cheese, and the collard greens. You get the catfish and whatever sides you want, and we could share?"

Anika tilted her head. "Deal."

Her eyes didn't leave his, and a sense of the familiar shadowed the table. They'd shared meals in a similar fashion in Venice, making sure to always order different items so they could sample a variety of food. One time she'd ordered the pumpkin gnocchi and he'd ordered the seafood vermicelli. Another time his meal had consisted of roasted lamb chops while she'd craved grilled fish. Despite all the time that had passed, it seemed only natural to do the same during this meal.

Moments later, they'd placed their orders and had beverages in front of them. As an appetizer, they shared an order of green tomatoes, fried with aged Parmesan cheese.

"How is it?" Anika asked, slicing into a tomato.

Reed finished chewing. "Delicious." He set down his fork. "I know I've said this before, but thanks again for helping with Brielle."

"I was happy to help. Now stop thanking me." Anika held up her glass of ginger ale. "To little girls with the lungs of an opera singer." She took a sip.

He laughed softly. The sound was warm and inviting, as if he were laughing at a private joke. It made her want to lean in and find out what the secret was. "You're in a good mood tonight."

It was true. Dating, especially the first few dates when a man and woman were initially feeling each other out, could be tense and quite nerve-wracking. That wasn't the case here. The initial nervousness didn't exist and a comfortable familiarity was firmly in place.

"I'm trying to be nice. Don't spoil it," Anika said.

"Okay, okay. I won't. I'm enjoying this moment, that's all."

Reed sipped from a bottle of Full Moon lager, watching her the entire time. "So tell me, what have you been up to during the past seven years or so? I mean, other than interior design."

Anika shrugged. "Nothing much. Work has consumed a lot of my time."

"What about boyfriends?"

The direct question made her skin tingle. "Alrighty then. Just come right out and ask the tough questions."

"Too personal?" he asked.

"I wasn't expecting that question until dessert. I haven't even had my meal yet. We're still on the appetizer."

"We can wait if you prefer, but it'll come up again."

"Hmm…then I'd rather bite the bullet and dive right in." Anika brushed a strand of hair from her brow. "Like I told you before, I'm not seeing anyone seriously. I've dated, of course. Lately I've met men through online sites."

He tapped a finger on the table. "How's that working out for you?"

"I've had good and bad experiences. Mostly good, but every now and again there's a bad one in the bunch." She shrugged.

"Any bad ones recently?"

She thought for a moment. "A few weeks ago I went out with a guy who was nice enough, but halfway through the dinner I knew he wasn't right for me."

"So this was a first date?"

"Yes."

"After one date, how can you be sure he wasn't right for you?"

"No spark."

His finger stopped tapping. "Oh. Gotta have spark. It's a lot more important than people think."

"Agreed." Anika dug her fork into a piece of tomato and

popped it into her mouth. He wasn't eating, his sharp blue eyes rested on her as he leaned back in the chair and gave her his undivided attention. "How about you? Are you dating?"

"Not since I moved here." He rubbed condensation from the outside of the bottle with his thumb. The same thumb he'd traced her lips with before he took her mouth in a hungry kiss.

Heat settled between her legs, and Anika cleared her throat, shifting to a more comfortable position in the chair. "No one at all?"

He smiled slightly. "Brielle's my priority. I haven't had the time or desire to date anyone seriously."

"But you want to?"

"Seriously. Casually. I'm fine either way. At the end of the day, my priority is Brielle."

"So you're telling me, since you moved here, you've been sitting at home twiddling your thumbs?" She couldn't imagine that. Reed was too passionate, too playful.

"I didn't say *that*."

"So there's been someone?" Her voice lowered. Anticipating his response shouldn't make her muscles tense. She shouldn't care so much about his answer.

His eyes looked steadily into hers. "A couple of women. Nothing serious. The right woman hasn't come along yet. Although, I think my luck might be changing."

"I see." She met his intense gaze head on. A hefty silence settled over the table and Anika reached for her glass, taking a large gulp. "Brielle's a lucky girl, to have such a dedicated father."

"I'm the lucky one. She's a good kid, sweet as can be. I just don't know what gets into her when she throws the tantrums, though. She's struggling, and I don't know how to help her." Brow furrowed, Reed stared down at the table.

"Do you think it's solely because her mother died?" Anika asked gently, not wanting to overstep her bounds.

Reed seemed inclined to talk. "Hell, I don't know what to think." He rubbed a hand across his brow. "Her grandmother took her to a therapist for a while, but he didn't think Brielle needed him. He insisted she was coping well, but I'm not so sure. When we first moved here, she was unhappy—kinda cranky but nothing too serious. Since I've been working from home a few days a week, she's been in a better mood. I think she just needed to know I'd be there, you know? But every now and again, she throws these tantrums—such as the one you saw the other day. Something's wrong. I don't think she's struggling with the loss of her mother. She may not fully understand, but she's accepted it. She knows her mommy won't be coming back. I think the tantrums are because she misses her family back in Dallas. What's strange is that she was fine at first. The tantrums started a couple of months ago, not long after we moved into the house."

"What do you think it means?"

He was quiet for a while as he pondered the question. "Maybe on some level Brielle understands the permanence of a house. It means that we're setting down roots and she won't be going back to Dallas, and when she talks to her grandmother, she thinks she won't see her again—just like she hasn't seen her mother again. I have another theory, but…I don't know." He shook his head, the frown deepening. "I'm still figuring out this father-thing. I'm never really sure if what I'm doing is right, but I try to put her first and hope everything else falls into place."

"That's all you can do."

"I should be doing more."

"You feel guilty for bringing her to Atlanta," Anika said quietly.

His gaze flicked up to her. "A little. I wasn't the"—he shifted in the seat—"best father when her mother, Layla, was alive, but I want the best for my daughter. Because of that, sometimes I'm not sure that bringing her here was the right decision. Maybe I'm being selfish."

"You're her father. You have every right to spend time with Brielle. She's young and this is all new. You have to give her time."

"Yeah. It's just that when she acts out, I'm not so sure time will change anything."

"On a daily basis, how does she behave?"

"She's a healthy, normal, happy kid."

"There's your answer." Anika smiled at him. "The problem isn't the location. The problem isn't you. Moving into a new house is a big change for a child, and maybe she does miss her grandmother, but you'll have to be patient. You've only lived in Atlanta for six or seven months. It hasn't been that long."

He laughed shortly. "Patience isn't exactly something I have in spades, as you can tell. But maybe I can cultivate that quality in myself."

"I think you're capable of it."

"Yeah?" He studied her, an odd little smile on his face.

Anika's cheeks heated and she played with the napkin in her lap. "Yeah."

"So how'd you get to be so smart?" He sipped his beer.

"It's not smarts. I'm speaking as someone who loved her father to death, and I don't regret one minute of our time together, even when we didn't see eye to eye. I wish he were alive and I could make more memories with him. Trust me, Brielle will come around. I'm confident."

"Tell me something, Anika." Reed leaned in. "Why hasn't some man swept you up already?"

"What?" Her stomach bottomed out. How many times had she heard the same type of question?

Why aren't you married?

You're a good woman. Are these men out here blind?

Why isn't there a ring on your finger already?

People thought those questions were compliments, but instead reminded her of how much she was lacking. She longed for a happy relationship with someone she loved and who loved her back, but her inferiority to other women was never far from her mind, and the reason she had to be so particular about the types of men she dated.

"You heard me." His voice lowered. "You're absolutely beautiful."

Anika never thought of herself in those terms. She was cute, and she'd even go so far as to say attractive on a good day, but beautiful was not a word she'd ever use to describe herself. He'd called her beautiful before, in the heat of passion, and she'd flushed at the wonder in his voice when he described her in those terms.

"You know you're beautiful, don't you? And sexy. You're sweet, good with kids, you know how to pick the perfect restaurant. It doesn't make sense." Reed narrowed his eyes. "I know what it is. Are you secretly a serial killer or something? You *seem* perfect, but there's something wrong with you. Am I right?"

Anika flinched involuntarily and her hands clenched in her lap. His teasing words were meant as a joke, but the comment almost unraveled her. Her situation—one that she'd learned to live with—on occasion managed to hurt like hell.

"Hey, what did I say?" Alarm filled Reed's voice.

Anika shook her head, staring down at her clenched fingers.

"Anika." He reached across the table, but she didn't take his hand.

"I'm fine." She pasted a smile on her face that she hoped appeared genuine. "As far as I know, there's nothing wrong with me."

She heard Emerson's voice again, telling her that was not the case.

You're broken.

85

Anika fought back the hurtful words by draining the contents of her glass. She squared her shoulders. "So, tell me about your job. What exactly does an accounting manager do?"

CHAPTER 12

*D*ammit.

After she'd made him feel so good, he'd made her feel bad.

The joke, which Reed now regretted, had shifted the conversation, and Anika's previously bright brown eyes now appeared dull and sad.

"The Continuum CPA Group specializes in offering accounting and business advisory services to small and medium-sized firms. My job includes basic tasks such as setting objectives and goal-setting. I audit the work of my staff, develop and train them, prepare policies and procedures, and make sure we stay compliant according to general accounting principles."

"Do you enjoy it?"

He nodded. "More than I thought I would. At my firm, one of the perks is that my position allows flexibility so I can spend time with my very own opera singer."

He smiled, and she did, too.

"If I had one complaint, it's that I have to attend more networking events. That's how I met Judge Evers. I'm starting to hate those things. Makes me miss being a staff accountant sometimes."

Anika brushed her hair off her shoulder. Reed wished he were sitting next to her so he could run his fingers through her hair and touch her bare skin.

"I'm surprised. I always thought of you as the outgoing type. I imagined you living in New York and having quite the active social life." She was getting back to normal, her eyes clearer, her voice sounding stronger and less strained.

"I did have an active social life. New York was crazy. Fun."

Too crazy. Too much fun. In retrospect, he'd been out of control for years. He'd partied hard and slept around. A starch-shirted accountant by day, but after hours, seeking some indefinable escape to settle his mind by engaging in activities that at twenty-nine years old now left him shamefaced.

He became a different man because of having to care for his daughter. A new man. She kept him busy and grounded, and for her sake, he'd changed.

He was certainly more responsible than his own father had been. His father lived on the west coast with his latest girlfriend half his age. Life with his dad had been a roller-coaster ride. They'd lived a bachelor lifestyle after his mother died—barely getting by but having what they considered to be a good life. He'd never learned responsibility from his dad, only how to have fun and live in the moment. On any given day, they'd hop in the car and start driving, going until they ran out of money. For a teenaged boy, those had been the best kind of adventures.

They'd moved around multiple times, been evicted twice, and one time lived in the car for two weeks. He loved his dad to death, but he'd been more of a frat brother than a father. He certainly hadn't taught him any parenting skills or how to be a responsible adult. He'd had to learn those things on his own. What he had taught him was what *not* to do. For Reed, that meant establishing stability in Brielle's life. No uncertainty allowed.

Their meals arrived, and as Anika had stated, the food was delicious. They ate every bite and ended dinner with healthy portions of peach cobbler and strong coffee.

Except for his joke, the night went exceptionally well. Conversation flowed easily, and he learned more about Anika than he did before. She talked a lot about her father, who'd passed before she entered college, and she had a strong relationship with her mother and brothers. From her description of her mother, they had similar personalities and tastes. Their similar taste in style was confirmed when she showed him a photo of her mother in her phone. She had the same light brown skin with golden undertones, and was dressed to the nines in a royal blue dress, large gold hat with a large rose, and matching bag—on her way to church. There was no doubt where Anika got her style from.

Reed didn't want to leave the restaurant, but he had to be considerate of Mrs. Miller's time. He paid for the meal, and they went outside into the balmy night air. He told the valet they'd get their own cars because he didn't want the night to end right then. He tipped the man and strolled with Anika toward her vehicle at the back of the lot, walking as slowly as he could. She walked slowly, too.

"Remember that moped ride in Venice?" he asked.

A soft smile came to her face. "How could I forget? I can't believe you convinced me to get on that thing."

"Whoa, wait a minute." Reed stopped. "I didn't convince you. You convinced me, remember?"

"That's not how I remember it."

"Well, let me refresh your memory, madam." He started walking again. "The night before, we ate dinner at that restaurant, the one the concierge recommended—down the alley behind the clothing store."

"I remember. We got so much food and that chicken dish was oh—so good. Just delicious." She sighed.

"At the end of our meal, you whipped out one of your ten thousand brochures, and that one was about moped rentals."

"I did not have ten thousand brochures."

"Damn near."

"And I didn't whip it out."

"Who's telling this story?"

She glared at him. "Fine. Proceed," she said, waving her hand with a flourish.

"As I was saying, you whipped out a brochure about moped rentals and said we should get one to explore the city. I asked if you'd ever ridden on a moped, and you said no. To which I said, it might not be a good idea for us to do, since neither one of us has ever ridden on one of those things. Any of this ringing a bell?"

She stopped at her car in the crowded lot. "Vaguely."

"Uh-huh." He side-eyed her but continued. "The next day, you brought up the same topic about mopeds after breakfast and badgered me about it."

Her mouth fell open and she propped her hands on her hips. "Wait a minute, now you're being completely ridiculous. Badgered you?"

"Badgered me," Reed confirmed. "I think you even hit me once to get me to fall in line with your demands."

She tossed her head back in laughter then. This was the Anika he remembered. Carefree. Spirited. "Unbelievable. You're making all of this up."

"I still have the scars," he muttered, rubbing an arm as if that's where she'd hit him.

"You need to take a polygraph," she said.

"So, after the physical and verbal abuse—"

"Oh my goodness." She hid her laughter behind her hand.

"—I finally agreed to rent the moped. You hopped on the back, and we spent the day exploring the city."

"Now that part is true."

"All of it is true."

"In an alternate universe."

He shrugged, absurdly pleased he could make her laugh and smile.

Her face partially in shadow, Anika tucked her hair behind an ear.

"We had fun that day," she said.

"Just that day?"

She fell silent, and he could hear the cars whizzing by on the street.

"Every day," she said quietly.

Emotion constricted his throat. Loss. Regret. Sweet memories. "You ever been back?"

She shook her head, gaze shifting away, as if she didn't want him to see the truth in her eyes. "I wanted to. Never took the time." She looked up at him from beneath her lashes, a look that made his chest clench with emotion. "You?"

"No, but I wouldn't mind going back."

Pressure built in his torso. He wanted to tell her how much he regretted not sharing his feelings in Venice. He regretted not following his heart and thinking neither of them was ready. But they were both older and still single, and the attraction was obviously still there. He experienced the tug every time she looked at him. Their chemistry hadn't dissipated one bit.

"You know what's crazy?" He ran his fingers through a few of the blonde strands that brushed her shoulders. Finally. As soft as he remembered. He saw it as a good sign that she didn't slap away his hand or move from his touch.

"What?"

"I didn't want to go back because I didn't think I could possibly enjoy myself as much as I did when I was there with you."

"Reed…" His name fell softly from her lips, whispered in the same tone as an urgent prayer. "It was a long time ago."

Spending time with her had been the perfect escape from the reality of his life and the tragedy of losing his mother at thirteen, which still managed to pummel him at random times. They'd been close, the way mothers and sons often are, and there were times when he missed her with a fierceness that made him weak. Three graduations—middle school, high school, and college—came and went without her there, and so did the birth of his child. Brielle would never know her paternal grandmother.

He'd gone to Venice because of her, hiding his grief behind smiles and a laid back attitude. Then he'd seen Anika, radiant and colorful in pink and purple—the Venetian sun shining down on her golden brown skin. She'd shaken him out of his funk. Now here she was for a second time—this time as he struggled with the challenge of being a single parent. Was it only coincidence that she had come along when he needed her again?

"Our trip wasn't that long ago, and I can't pretend that I don't feel what I feel. That's impossible." He cupped her exposed shoulder and stepped closer, leaving very little space separating them. She tilted back her head to look up at him. "If I could go back in time and redo the day I left, I would. I'd tell you that I wanted to stay and admit that I was scared. It's no excuse, but I'm sorry I hurt you. I don't think I've ever regretted anything as much as I regret leaving you that day."

Tears surfaced in her eyes and she bit down on her lower lip. He continued talking because he knew he was getting through to her.

"Every single day and every single night we spent together have stayed with me. You haven't forgotten, either, have you? This is going to sound like a bullshit line, but I still miss your laugh. That's one of the most vivid memories I have of us. The two of us laughing, over dinner or in bed. You helped me a lot. I don't think you know how much."

Her face crumbled for a second before she got her emotions under control. "You helped me, too. More than you know. I'd been at a low point after Emerson dumped me."

"Lucky for me, Emerson was a fool." He traced her bottom lip with his thumb. He wanted to kiss her so badly. The constant need to do so had punctuated his thoughts every few minutes throughout the evening. "Do you believe in fate?"

She closed her eyes.

"I do," Reed continued. "I don't think it was chance that we ran into each other thousands of miles away on another continent. I don't think it was chance that I met Judge Evers at a function and got a referral to Davenport Design Studio. That was fate, bringing us together again."

Anika opened her eyes, and he met her gaze unflinchingly, imploring her to accept the truth of his words.

Reed rested a hand on the roof of the car and bent his head. He was so close now, he saw the individual lashes of her eyes. She pressed a hand against his chest to keep him at bay.

"You can't deny this attraction between us, Anika. This… thing. I don't even know how to describe it. Venice was incredible. Fantastic. I've never forgotten our time together. Have you?"

"No." She took a shaky breath. "Reed, we shouldn't. I can't." Her voice shook. "It was so long ago and everything is different. We can't work."

"I disagree."

She was trying to talk herself out of it, but nothing she said would make him change his mind. He'd screwed up by letting her walk away once before. He didn't plan on making the same mistake again.

Their eyes met, and in an instant, he knew that he would kiss her, and he knew that she would let him.

He kissed her shoulder, taking his time and breathing her in. The scent of her perfume and skin were a subtle aphrodisiac. God help him, he wanted her so badly, every nerve in his body screamed with the need.

Slipping a hand to the back of her neck and beneath the heavy weight of her hair, Reed licked his lips. "I can still taste you," he whispered hoarsely.

He grazed her mouth with his. It was just enough to give him a taste of strawberry lip gloss. When she inhaled sharply, he took the opportunity to seize her parted lips.

CHAPTER 13

*R*eed swallowed Anika's gasp and soft moan, winding an arm around her waist and drawing her tight to his body. Her soft curves pressed into him, and he swelled in his pants. The longing he'd experienced since seeing her again came to a head, pushing up with the force of a geyser and fixing his lips harder onto hers.

He hadn't planned for this to happen. He'd truly meant to thank her for the help with his daughter and spend some much-desired time in her presence, but going out to dinner and talking about the past simply made him unable to resist the lure of her mouth and the invitation of her dark eyes. His need had taken charge. It was an unstoppable force that broke down his willpower as easily as a battering ram would a canvas wall.

One knee shifted between her thighs as he pushed her into the cool car. He was moving too fast. Wanting her too much. But he didn't know how to stop. Certainly not when she purred and allowed him to slide in his tongue. Her soft kisses prompted him to swipe at the interior with eager enthusiasm. She sucked on his tongue, slipping her fingers through the hairs at the nape of his neck and sending heated tingles down his spine.

He kissed her jaw and swept her hair aside to suck on her skin, listening to the breathy moan of pleasure that escaped. The scent of her overwhelmed him and charged heat through his blood as he flicked the tip of his tongue across the racing pulse at her throat and tasted the slightly salty flavor of her skin.

Boldly, he shifted his hand inside the split of her skirt and lifted her foot from the pavement, angling her knee to his hip. Another gasp fell from her lips with a murmured *oh god* as he ground his hips between her legs. His hand was inside her panties now, rubbing at her swollen clit and sliding through the slippery wetness until her head fell back.

"Damn," he muttered, watching her give herself over to the pleasure of his touch.

Her hips undulated, rubbing her sex against the palm of his hand, her face twisted into an expression of tortured pleasure as she bit down on her bottom lip and breathed heavily through her nose.

Reed nipped at her neck. "Don't fight it. Please don't fight it. I want to hear you."

He slid two fingers into her and stroked. Then he kissed her, hard. A fierce, intense melding of the mouths that had her sinking her fingers into his hair.

He didn't let up. His fingers continued a steady stroke between her legs. And then, with a gentle squeeze of her clit, she shattered, gasping and pressing her face to his chest to keep from crying out loud, her hips working feverishly against his hand to capture the last remnants of ecstasy.

Reed gently kissed her temple. Then he moved to her ear and down to her neck. "Sweet, sweet Anika."

She kept her face hidden against his chest, breathing heavily, while Reed slipped both arms around her waist and held her close. His own body begged for release, but he ignored the discomfort of his rigid hard-on, concentrating on Anika and the fact that he was holding her again.

From a distance he heard laughter, and at the corner of his eye a trio of restaurant guests strolled through the parking lot. The group sent a cursory glance in their direction before exiting the lot to the hotel nearby.

Reed studied Anika's bent head. "Talk to me."

His body burned for her. He wished he could scoop her up and whisk her away from there, but he remained silent, awaiting a response.

"I don't want to get hurt."

Reed brushed the back of his fingers down her arm. "I won't hurt you." She finally returned her gaze to him, and the wounded expression in her eyes cut him straight to the bone. "When you look at me like that, it kills me."

A slight tremor disturbed the line of her lips. "I don't know what to think. Maybe you're trying to recapture the past, but what we had has come and gone. I don't think it's possible to recreate that."

"So you admit that there was something deeper between us?" Acknowledgement. That was a start, at least.

"Yes. *Was* something between us. Past tense."

"We can recreate that feeling again. That closeness that we shared."

She let out an off-pitch laugh. "But why? What difference does it make? You walked away before."

"What happened between us was unexpected. I planned to explore the city that I had heard my mother talk about for years. I never for one minute thought I'd see you and enjoy myself the way I did. I messed up, big time. I let you go. I won't do that again. I want a chance with you, a real chance. You can't deny we're good together."

"Chemistry is not the same as being good together. There are things you don't know about me. Maybe once you find out, you won't be so open-minded." She hugged herself.

"I want to know everything—the good, the bad, the ugly. And I want you to know everything about me."

He tilted up her chin to look him in the eyes. "Listen, I'm not going anywhere this time. I'm in for the long haul. I want you to be comfortable with this, too. We'll take our time and get to know each other. We're different people than we were seven years ago. And I'd love for you to spend more time with my daughter and get to know her. It's obvious Brielle has taken to you, and you did a much better job of calming her down than I ever have."

He still saw hesitation in her eyes. She was keeping the walls up, but he suspected the reason for doing so wasn't only because he'd hurt her. Something else kept her guarded.

"I won't push. Tonight was only supposed to be about thanking you, but I can't deny I want more." His voice lowered to a husky whisper. "I want you. Give me a chance and let me make it up to you and prove you can trust me. Will you at least try?"

She didn't answer right away, staring into his eyes as if seeking the truth.

Finally, she nodded. "I'll try."

With utmost relief, Reed rested his forehead against hers. That's all he could ask of her for now, but knew he had his work cut out for him. Luckily, he was up for the challenge. Venice was not a fluke. The referral to Davenport Design Studio was not by chance.

Fate had brought them together again, and this time, he would not waste his chance.

CHAPTER 14

"So, what do you think?" Anika bit her thumbnail, closely watching Reed as he reviewed the sketches and images she brought to their weekday lunch. They were eating sandwiches on the first floor of the office building where he worked.

She finally put together all the elements for Brielle's room and had presented them, but trying to gauge his reaction was not the only reason she kept her eyes on him. He looked striking in a navy suit, navy tie, and pale blue shirt that brought out the blue in his eyes. She didn't miss the fact that other women paid him an extraordinary amount of attention, trying to be surreptitious but failing miserably when they kept their gazes on his handsome face much longer than appropriate.

For Brielle's room Anika envisioned a beautiful display of butterflies adhered to the wall above the bed. The manufacturer she sourced them from assured her the adhesive was temporary, and as Brielle grew out of her butterfly phase, they could easily be removed without damaging the painted wall.

"Do you think she'll like it?" She was impatient and desperately wanted to hear his thoughts.

"She'll love it."

"Really?" She put a lot of thought into the design and picking the colors for the bed linens and curtains. The room should reflect Brielle's personality and be a place where the little girl looked forward to spending time.

"I can't see how she won't love falling asleep below all these butterflies every night."

Anika rested her chin on her hand. "And when your cousin builds the window seat, that will give her a new place to store her toys."

His cousin, Ryan, built custom furniture and had already been by to measure the space.

"He said he can get to that this week." Reed took her hand and brought her knuckles to his lips. Her skin tingled where his mouth touched. "I can't wait to see the finished product." He was talking about the house but the soft expression in his eyes melted her insides.

"The whole house is almost finished," Anika said.

"Hmmm. So I'll have to come up with excuses to spend time with you."

"You won't have to do that."

"No excuses necessary?" His thumb gently rubbed across her knuckles.

"None at all."

They leaned in to each other at the same time and kissed. She could kiss him all day. His lips were soft and delicious, and the physical contact never failed to warm her belly.

They spent the rest of lunch making plans to get together and finalized the details for the house. When the alarm on Reed's phone went off signaling the end of his break, Anika's shoulders slumped. Their time together was too short.

"Got to run back to the office," Reed said regretfully.

"I'm glad we got the chance to spend a little time together." Even though she was attracted to Reed and wanted to get inside his pants, she nonetheless hoped for more moments similar to this one, where they could simply enjoy each other's company. And there was no pressure. He seemed to want to just be with her, which made her fall deeper under his spell.

"I'm glad we did, too. You have any appointments this afternoon?"

Anika shook her head. "I'm working in the office all afternoon, and um, I have a meeting with Laura."

"About becoming an owner?" Reed asked.

"That's the impression she gave me." A nervous flutter flickered through her insides.

"Are you ready?"

Reed massaged her shoulder, and the gentle squeeze and roll motion helped relax her anxiety somewhat.

"I've been ready for a long time. I just need her to officially make me an offer."

"It'll happen. Keep your thoughts positive." He reassured her with a smile and a gentle squeeze of her shoulder.

They emptied their trays and before parting ways, Reed pulled Anika in for another quick kiss. By the time she arrived at her car, she could barely remember walking to the parking lot. She was so drunk on Reed, she could only assume that she'd floated there.

* * *

WHEN ANIKA ENTERED THE OFFICE, Jasmine was sitting on the edge of the desk and laughing hysterically as Edgar made exaggerated motions with his hands during the course of telling what appeared to be a very interesting story.

She greeted them and headed for the staircase.

"Mrs. Winthrop called," Jasmine said.

Anika paused with one hand on the handrail and groaned. "Oh, no. What was the call about?" The Winthrop project had wrapped up weeks ago. There had been no complaints, but no glowing reviews, either, and no response to the customary follow up message left to ensure clients were one hundred percent satisfied.

"She said something about a beach house needing a redesign." Jasmine raised an eyebrow above her glasses.

Anika raised an eyebrow, too. "Did she?"

Jasmine nodded vigorously. "Yes. I guess we were worried about nothing. She must be happy if she's calling to have us work on another home."

"I guess so." Sometimes you couldn't tell with clients, but this was definitely good news.

Edgar jumped into the conversation with a smug grin. "She must be happy with *our* work. Me and my guys did a helluva good job over there. Tell the truth."

"Oh, of course," Anika agreed, climbing the stairs. "My education and creativity are secondary to your demolition ability. Why, this whole firm would be nothing without you and your guys."

"I sense sarcasm," Edgar called after her.

"And you've got great intuition," Anika continued.

She killed time in her office by returning Mrs. Winthrop's call and discussing the details of the new project, a beach house in Hilton Head. After a lengthy conversation to discuss her needs, she wrapped up the call in time for her meeting with Laura.

Taking a deep breath, she made her way to her boss's office and was waved in while Laura was on the phone. Anika crossed her legs and waited, listening as Laura finessed a supplier into giving her a bigger discount than usual, her voice dripping with warmth and pure Southern charm.

When Laura finished the call, she folded her hands on the desk and gave Anika her undivided attention. "I'm not going to beat around the bush. We've talked about this in the past, and after much thought, I want to offer you a fifteen percent stake in Davenport Design Studio. Are you still interested?"

Anika remained momentarily speechless but kept her face as neutral as she could, hands clasped in her lap. Meanwhile, her insides turned perfectly executed backflips. Laura had offered her a greater stake than expected. She assumed she would offer around five percent or even ten percent, max. Fifteen percent was a wonderful surprise.

"I am still very interested, and fifteen percent is perfect."

Laura's smile widened. "Well, hot dog! I was hoping you'd say that. I'll have my attorney draw up the papers for your review."

They spoke for a few more minutes about the dollar amount and other details. Anika would call her business broker to help her negotiate the particulars, but had already secured conditional financing, and with her personal funds could easily close the deal.

She and Laura shook hands, and Anika raced up the stairs to her office. She slammed the door and let out a silent scream, then danced around the room before collapsing into her chair.

"It's happening. Oh my goodness." She snatched up the phone and plugged in the first three digits of Reed's number. Then stopped.

She hung up. She stared at the phone.

He was the first person she thought of calling. Not her mother, who'd be proud, or her cousin, Ronnie. The first person she couldn't wait to tell the good news was Reed Stewart.

It's okay, Anika. She pressed her forehead to her fist.

Was it really okay?

She was falling for him. She loved his warm smile, especially when he did that cute thing where only one side of his mouth lifted into it. It was crookedly adorable and sexy at the same time. His sense of humor never failed to make her laugh or lift her spirits. His hotness—lord, that man was fine in a suit!

She laughed to herself. "It's okay, Anika." This time she said the words aloud, giving herself a mini pep talk. She picked up the phone and dialed his number. Funny how she already knew all his numbers by heart.

"Hello."

Anika let the warmth of his voice wash over her. Her heart went berserk and filled with a sensation she couldn't adequately describe.

"Hi." Her voice came out much softer than intended and she couldn't complete another word. She was simply over-whelmed by him and the emotions he evoked.

"Don't keep me in suspense. What happened? How did your meeting go?"

She perked up and cleared her throat. "The meeting was short and sweet but went well. She's having the papers drawn up. You're talking to a future business owner."

Reed let out a loud whoop. "Congratulations! Sweetheart, I'm so proud of you."

Anika sank into the back of the chair, basking in his supportive enthusiasm. "I can't believe it."

"I can. All your hard work is paying off." He paused. "How about you join me and Brielle for ice cream this week-end, as sort of a pre-celebration celebration until you sign the actual contract?"

"I think that's a great idea."

"I'll pick you up on Saturday."

They talked for a few more minutes, and after they hung up, Anika wished it was the weekend already.

CHAPTER 15

"*J*ust a few more steps."

With one hand over Brielle's eyes, Reed steered his daughter into the bedroom where Anika had put the finishing touches only minutes before. She stood aside as they entered, scanning the room one more time to make sure she hadn't missed anything.

The room had come together nicely. A collage of colorful 3D butterflies were attached to the wall behind Brielle's bed, and Anika had suspended another ten out of reach from the ceiling, but directly over the pillow so they were the first thing Brielle saw when she woke up in the morning. The outlet covers had been replaced with butterfly switch plates, and the bed was made with pillows and linens in pastel colors that matched the new curtains. A comfy armchair gave Reed a place to sit on the nights he checked in on Brielle, and she'd gotten rid of Brielle's old toy box after Ryan installed the window seat, arranging the stuffed animals so they could lounge on top of it.

Reed removed his hand. "Open your eyes."

Brielle's mouth fell open, and she jumped up and down.

"Is this for me?" She looked back at her father, eyes wide as if she couldn't believe it.

"All for you, baby."

"I love it!" Two seconds later, Brielle burst into tears and pressed her tiny fists to her eyes.

Reed dropped to his knees and pulled her into a hug. "Ah, baby, why are you crying?"

"Everything is so pretty." Brielle sniffled. "I love it so much."

Watching Brielle cry happy tears against her father's chest, Anika had to blink back her own tears. She'd expected joy but hadn't foreseen this overflow of emotion from the little girl.

Reed rubbed his daughter's back, cradling her close until her sobbing quieted.

"Thank you, Daddy."

He pushed his daughter's hair out of her face. "You don't have to thank me, baby. I'd do anything for you." He kissed Brielle's eyelids and swiped away the remnants of her tears with his thumbs. Lifting her into his arms, he said, "Miss Anika did all the work. What do you say?"

"Thank you, Miss Anika."

"You're welcome, sweetie."

Reed and Anika simply gazed at each other for a moment. He couldn't hide the utter appreciation in his eyes, which made her feel particularly sentimental that she'd been a part of making them both so happy. Hands down, the best part of her job was the awe and joy on her clients' faces after a transformation of their living space.

"I guess now we can finish dinner," Reed said.

"I'll meet you downstairs. I'm going to check the other rooms."

The house was finally complete. Anika walked through each room, taking in all the changes. For the most part, the project had moved along smoothly, with only a few hiccups. It helped that Reed was so accommodating.

The neutral paint added warmth and needed color to the walls. The furnishings beautified the home with carefully curated pieces that added comfort and style, while allowing for the relaxed environment Reed preferred. And now Brielle's room had satisfied not only Reed, but his little girl, as well.

The only outstanding item needed was a piece for the empty wall in the living room. Reed had rejected her suggestions thus far, but Anika hadn't given up on her quest to find the perfect wall hanging that would tie in the blue and earth tones in the color scheme.

"What's for dinner?" she asked, walking into the kitchen. Reed stood at the stove, stirring a pot with a wooden spoon. The food smelled divine.

Brielle sat on her haunches on a stool at the island, her elbows resting on the cool granite top. Adorable with her long curly hair pouring down her back in loose curls, she wore a black T-shirt that said *Playdate Material* in silver script. In the past few weeks since she'd been spending more time with them, she'd learned from Reed that Brielle fell for shirts with writing on them, even though she couldn't read yet.

"Pasghetti and meatballs. It's my favorite," she said.

"Smells delicious," Anika said.

Brielle nodded vigorously. "Daddy makes good pasghetti."

"Need any help?" Anika asked.

"I'm almost done. I'm taking care of my ladies tonight."

The inside of her chest warmed at the words, and when Reed looked over his shoulder and winked at her, Anika blushed. With tax season over, they were able to spend more time together, but he still had to juggle caring for his daughter. Along with Mrs. Miller and a babysitter in the neighborhood, his cousins proved to be convenient alternatives in a pinch.

In addition to their evening jaunts to the movies, dinner,

or some other engagement, she and Reed squeezed in more lunches. With more flexibility in her schedule, they tended to meet at the deli on the first floor of the Continuum building, or she'd swing by the house to dine on the delicious paninis Mrs. Miller made when he worked from home.

Then, every night after he'd put Brielle to bed, Reed called and they talked for at least an hour, about nothing and everything—catching up on the past and getting gossip on old acquaintances from their college days.

"I can't wait to taste your spaghetti. I hope the food lives up to the hype from your biggest cheerleader."

Reed laughed. "She's definitely my biggest cheerleader. Did I ever tell you about my struggles with her hair?"

"No." Anika sat on one of the stools.

After a quick taste of the sauce, Reed sprinkled in a pinch of salt and resumed stirring. "I didn't have a clue how to style her hair. My cousin's wife was a lifesaver. She took me to Target and showed me all these products for women with curly hair." He set down the spoon and leaned his back against the counter, folding his arms across his chest. "Did you know there's a line called Mixed Chicks?"

Anika laughed. "Yes, I did."

"I was overwhelmed by the choices, but Shawna, my cousin's wife, she was really patient with me. I pulled in Mrs. Miller, too. We tried a few products, and Shawna showed us how to detangle and style Brielle's hair." He laughed to himself. "One day I was doing her hair, and her braid was crooked. I wanted to give up. You know what my daughter said to me?"

"What?"

"Do you remember what you said, Brielle?" The love in his eyes was evident when he looked at his daughter.

"You can do it, Daddy. I believe in you." Brielle grinned.

"That's right. You made sure Daddy didn't give up." As

he became emotional, Reed's jaw tightened. "So I started over, and I did it."

Anika smiled at him and then looked at Brielle's hair. "Now you're an old pro."

"If you think that's good, wait until you see my cornrows."

"You do cornrows?"

"Don't sound so surprised. I'm not half bad." He drained the spaghetti into a colander. "We're eating on the deck tonight. If you don't mind, could you grab the plates from the cabinet and help me take the dishes out to the table?"

"I don't mind at all."

They spread out the food family style on the outdoor table —meatballs in a rich burgundy sauce, spaghetti bathed in olive oil and brightened with lemon zest, garlic bread, and steamed asparagus.

Each one of them wolfed the food down and cleaned their plates, including Brielle, who ate a hearty amount for someone so small. Her animated chatter and giggles filled the evening air as the sun went down. Watching Brielle and Reed together, it was obvious how much they adored each other. He patiently answered all her questions and listened attentively as she described her time at the park and a visit to the children's museum in painstaking detail.

When dinner was over, Anika sat on the den floor with Brielle and helped her build a castle with LEGOs, while Reed filled the dishwasher.

"Do you want me to put this here?" Anika asked, holding up one of the pieces. Brielle was very particular about what went where, so she was careful to ask each and every time.

"Um, no." A frown lodged between the little girl's eyes as she surveyed their work so far. "I'm going to put this one here, and you put that one over there, got it?"

Anika hid her smile so as not to undermine the solemn nature of their task. "Got it."

Reed came into the room holding the cordless phone.

"Brielle, Grandma's on the phone."

His daughter's face went from contemplative to sullen.

"What's the matter?" Reed asked.

Instead of answering, Brielle jumped up and launched onto Anika's lap, burying her face in her chest. Anika squeezed her tight, lightly brushing her hair with her hand, and stared up at Reed in bewilderment.

"I'll be right back," he said, and disappeared with the phone.

"Hey, sweetie, what's wrong?" Gentle prodding did nothing to nudge an answer from the little girl.

A few minutes later, Reed came back into the room and got down on the floor in front of Anika and his daughter, who still hid her face.

"Hey, there. What's wrong, honey? Talk to me." He brushed aside a swathe of hair so he could see the side of her face. Brielle didn't respond. He opened his arms. "Come here."

With her head bent low, Brielle slipped from Anika's lap and stood in front of her father. He tilted up her chin with one finger. "What's wrong? Does talking to Grandma make you sad?"

She nodded and then fell into his arms.

"All right. You don't have to talk to her right now, okay?" He rubbed her back and kissed her forehead. "Want to dance with me?"

"Yes," Brielle said softly.

They stood and Reed turned on the stereo. As the doo wop hit "Travelin' Man" poured out of the speakers, Anika moved to the sofa. Reed and Brielle moved in time to the music, in what appeared to be a choreographed dance they'd done before. It was the cutest thing she'd ever seen. Reed treated his daughter with such tenderness and care, her heart melted.

"You have to dance with Miss Anika now, Daddy," Brielle said when the song ended.

"I do? You think she'll want to dance with me?" He slanted a glance in Anika's direction.

Brielle came over to the sofa. "Do you want to dance with my daddy? He's a good dancer."

Anika suspected that for this little girl, there was nothing her father couldn't do well. "I would love to," she said.

"We've got to do what the young lady says," Reed teased, extending a hand.

She went to him and he pulled her close with one arm around her waist as "I Only Have Eyes for You," by the Flamingoes came through the speakers.

Their bodies glided across the floor in time to the music. "I hope you're having fun. I know we can't really talk with her here—or do anything else."

"I'm enjoying myself. I love spending time with Brielle," Anika quipped.

"I think I'm jealous." Reed turned them in a slow circle, laughter in his eyes. "She likes you a lot."

"I like her a lot."

"I like you a lot."

Anika's heart raced. "I like you a lot, too."

He rubbed his palm up and down her back, and her body came alive. She let the fingers of her right hand trail through the curly hairs at his neck as she gazed into his yes. They still hadn't made love, temporarily settling for amorous kisses and heavy petting—but nothing like the night at Paschal's, and her libido was in protest at being unsatisfied. It wouldn't be so bad if Reed wasn't the affectionate type. He thought nothing of touching and kissing her. Anika returned the constant contact, building the frustration to the boiling point.

"Are you free Friday night?" Reed asked.

"Are you?"

"I can be." He lowered his voice. "Shawna told me whenever I need a break, I was welcome to let Brielle spend the night. I think I might cash in that favor this weekend. So what do you think?"

Anika's body swayed with his. "That's a good idea, but I'm attending a cocktail party at city hall at six, and then I'm going to an art stroll to source art for clients."

"Care for some company at the art stroll?"

"I don't hate that idea."

"In that case, I'll cancel the limo and chartered plane I had rented to take us to New York for the night."

"My, my. You had big plans."

"Yeah, but since you have that art stroll, let's just stay in town and have some adult conversation and do other adult things."

Anika laughed softly, a tremble of anticipation filling her stomach. "You're just full of great ideas, aren't you?"

"I try." His eyes sparkled with amusement.

"My turn!" Brielle wedged her body between them and forced them apart. Anika returned to the sofa and basked in the warmth of Reed's smile as he looked over his daughter's head at her. She smiled back, heart full and excitement bubbling up inside her.

The pain had melted away and hesitation was a ghost from the past. Part of her wanted to slow down the speed with which she and Reed were moving forward, but another part knew it was impossible—that there was no way to ignore the magnitude of her emotional response to him. Their connection was undeniable and had survived the years they'd been apart. She knew she was taking a risk but dived in anyway, heart first.

Hoping, and praying, that she was not making a mistake this time.

CHAPTER 16

*W*ho counted down the hours until she saw a man? Anika Taylor did.

The reception at city hall concluded earlier than expected, so she arrived half an hour early to the appointed gallery where she and Reed agreed to meet. She was nervous. Probably because with Brielle spending the night at her cousins' house, tonight was a turning point. They teetered on the edge of a decision that would change them both for good.

The art stroll took place every second Friday of the month in the Castleberry Hill historic arts district. Not only did the local shops and galleries open their doors to the visitors descending on the neighborhood, artists came from out of town for the exposure. The additional foot traffic meant patrons and vendors buzzed throughout the street, and food trucks lining the avenue offered food options that could be enjoyed while strolling about.

Scoping out the interior of the gallery, she didn't see Reed anywhere and proceeded to check out the paintings. She'd made her way back to the front of the gallery when Reed sauntered in, his tall frame dominating as he stood on the threshold for several seconds, searching for her. Once spotting her, he came over, his eyes filled with warmth as his gaze caressed her face.

If it were possible to make someone melt simply by looking at them, Reed would leave puddles of melted females in his wake everywhere his feet tread. Taking her hand, he closed the gap between them with a gentle tug.

"Hi." He lifted her hand to his mouth.

Anika's breath caught and held before releasing again. "Hi."

He bit his bottom lip, eyes lowered to half-mast as he skimmed her body in the figure-hugging black dress. The neckline boldly dipped between her breasts and showed ample cleavage. She'd styled her hair in loose curls and wore more makeup than usual, which included red lips and smoky eyeshadow.

"You look incredible. How am I supposed to concentrate on the art in the galleries when I have a spectacular work of art right beside me?"

Anika giggled, warmth heating her cheeks. She'd taken great care with her appearance, and his reaction was exactly what she'd hoped for.

"You keep talking like that, and you might get lucky tonight."

Reed's eyes darkened and a predatory smile skated across his lips. "In that case..."

Shoving him with a laugh, Anika shook her head. "We're here to look at art. I let you join me, but remember I'm also working."

"Oh right, right." Reed's fingers brushed hers, and she leaned in, forgetting for a minute that they were in a gallery filled with patrons. He simply had that effect—he drew her in and made her forget her surroundings.

Their fingers laced together. Her hand fit comfortably in his warm clasp—as snug and secure as lambskin gloves. Touching him, holding hands, wasn't awkward in the least.

They walked through the gallery hand in hand.

"This is nice." Reed pointed at a large painting.

"The artist is from South Carolina." Anika kept tabs on him via social media and had been anxious to see his work in person. The painting was imbued with eye-catching reds, greens, and browns. She filed away the image to retrieve at a later date for a client.

"What do you think about this for the living room? Or something similar?" Reed asked.

Wrinkling her nose, Anika shook her head. "You need a piece that better brings together the room's neutral colors. Something subtler. How about...oh, how about that one." She pointed to another painting. It was of a man standing in a boat, moored next to an embankment. The artist had done such an excellent job, the blue-green water appeared to ripple on the canvas as it flowed beneath the white bridge.

"Remind you of anything?" Reed asked.

"Yes."

They didn't need to say another word or add additional detail. Their thoughts were perfectly in tune.

"I'm going to get it," Reed said.

"Now?"

"Yes. Before someone else does. I think it would be perfect for that empty space on the wall in the living room. It fits the decor, right?"

"It does."

"No time like the present."

They tracked down a salesperson and in very short order, a *Sold* sticker was placed on the painting, Reed paid for it, and gave the woman his information for delivery.

"Where to next?" He tucked Anika's hand back into his.

"Follow me."

They took their time browsing the other galleries, and because Anika knew a few of the gallery owners, she talked to them about undiscovered artists or new pieces that had arrived since her last visit. She also took photos whenever she saw a piece that could potentially work in a client's home, or if it was a work of art Davenport Design Studio could keep in their small showroom for future projects.

One of her favorite spots was the energy and vibrancy of No Mas Hacienda. The building housed a restaurant serving Mexican cuisine, a tequila tasting room, and an artisan market stocked with handmade goods—silver jewelry, masks, pottery, basket lights hanging from the ceiling, and fantastical creatures carved from the sacred copal tree and painted with intricate Zapotec symbols.

By the time they finished walking around, they'd worked up an appetite and joined the people crowded around the food trucks.

Anika ordered three tacos from a Mexican food vendor, and Reed chose BBQ pork ribs with a side of wedge fries. He sat on a window ledge outside a closed clothing store.

"Come here," he said, pulling Anika between his legs. "Sit."

"You want me to sit on you?" she said, playfully being difficult.

"Yes, I want you to sit on me." He smiled up at her.

"You promise there won't be any funny business?"

"I can't promise that. But sit anyway."

She eased onto his lap, and he moaned. She popped up. "Reed!"

He chuckled. "Sit, woman."

Anika settled her bottom on his thigh, wiggling more than necessary to get comfortable.

"Now you're playing with fire," he muttered, winding an arm around her waist and tugging her back to his chest.

"There are children out here," Anika warned, giggling.

"Then behave before you make me embarrass myself." He used his nose to brush aside her hair and kissed her behind the ear.

Anika angled away, but in doing so knocked over his bottle of beer sitting on the ledge beside him. The glass shattered and frothy liquid darkened the sidewalk as it crept toward the street.

"Look at what you did."

"Oops." Anika bit her lip. "Here, you can have some of mine." She lifted her beer to his mouth and he tilted his head back, swallowing a gulp.

"Thank you."

"It's the least I could do," she said softly.

"Tastes better than mine."

"It's the same beer," Anika pointed out.

"But your lips have been on that bottle."

Goodness, this man.

They gazed into each other's eyes, and the buildings and people around them receded from view and ceased to exist. They were the only two people in the world, and Anika's heart swelled in the perfection of that moment, where there was only she and Reed and the magic between them.

"Well, hello Reed!"

The vaguely familiar voice caused Anika to break eye contact. Her stomach tumbled uneasily when she saw the petite dark-haired woman coming toward them. Dharma looked like the perfect mother, with her hair pulled away from her face by a white cloth headband, pushing her son in a stroller and her daughter walking along beside her.

"How are you? Anika, right? The designer?" Her voice and tone were friendly, but Dharma's eyes were expressly confused.

"Yes."

"Your hair is different." Her gaze dropped to Anika's exposed cleavage and her smile became tighter.

Anika shifted with the intention of standing, but Reed's arm around her waist tightened and prohibited her from moving. "Taking the kids on a little outing, I see," he said.

Dharma's smile became more genuine when she addressed Reed. "Yes, and they have been cranky, cranky, cranky all night long." She sighed dramatically. "But I think it's important to expose children to the arts. Speaking of which, where's little Miss Brielle? Don't tell me you left her at home and she's missing out on all this culture." Her gaze fell to Anika again, this time more accusatory. She clearly blamed Anika for Brielle not being there.

"She's at a sleepover with her cousins," Reed replied.

"Oh. A sleepover. Well, I guess everyone needs a break every now and again."

"Yes, it's convenient to have a support system in place so I can take the occasional break and indulge in adult activities."

Dharma's eyebrow lifted a fraction. "As parents, we have to be careful that we don't allow ourselves to be distracted by...outside forces. As you know, my children are my priority." She smiled tightly. "I'll leave you to your adult *activities*." Anika could practically see the air quotes around the emphasized word. "It was nice seeing you. Anika." With a curt nod, she walked away.

"I guess I won't be getting any referrals from her after all," Anika murmured, watching Dharma stalk down the street with a stiff spine.

"Why do you say that?"

"She obviously has a crush on you and sees me as the enemy."

"You think so?"

"I know so. She probably thinks I'm leading you astray and causing you to forego your proper role as a father." Anika bit into her taco and chewed. "And don't act like you don't know she likes you."

"I've never encouraged her." He nudged her neck with his lips. "Do you know who I have encouraged, though?"

"Who?"

"You." Reed rested his forehead to her temple. His hand slid to her hip and then covered her thigh.

"Reed, we're in public," Anika said in a breathy voice, even as her thighs opened a fraction.

"Then let's go somewhere private." His shaft hardened beneath her bottom.

"What did you have in mind?" Anika asked.

"Adult activities." He kissed the corner of her mouth, pulling her closer. "Only if you want to, Anika." His words were amenable, but she heard the edge of hunger in his voice.

Anika cupped his hard jaw with her free hand and ran her thumb over the soft bristles on his chin. "I want to."

There was nothing else she wanted more at that moment.

CHAPTER 17

*T*hey fell onto the bed, mouths eagerly fused together as they fumbled with zippers and buttons. Reed shrugged out of his jacket and shirt and unceremoniously lifted Anika's dress over her head, dropping it onto the pile on the floor. All she wore underneath was a pair of black, full lace boy shorts that gave him pause.

Swearing softly, his heated gaze swept her body. He trailed a hand down the middle of her torso, awakening the sensitive flesh of her breasts with a series of sparks that made her nipples harden even more than they already had.

"I'm so glad you came into my life again." He said the words in a semi-detached way, not to her, but almost to himself. "You have no idea how much."

He reclaimed her mouth, and Anika came alive in his arms. Warm lips caressed hers, first plucking at the full bottom one and then nibbling at each corner. But it wasn't enough. She wrapped her arms around his neck and sealed their lips together, demanding a proper kiss. Wrapping one leg around his waist, she grinded her pelvis against his hard shaft to ease the ache that echoed through her loins unrestricted.

She tried not to go too fast, but excitement twisted in her stomach. It felt as if she'd been waiting for this particular kiss for years—the prelude to a meeting of the minds and bodies, resulting in a rapid pulse and goose bumps on her arms. Their tongues twisted around each other in a seductive dance. The dizzying exploration left her drunk on passion and her excited heart hitting against her ribs in an out-of-control cadence.

Reed lifted his head and cradled her face in his big hands. With naked hunger in his eyes, he said, "It's different this time, Anika. Do you understand?"

She nodded. "I do."

The first time they'd fallen into a whirlpool of emotion by accident, unexpectedly. This time, both she and he knew what they were getting themselves into. They were making a conscious decision to risk their hearts, and for the first time in a long time she wasn't afraid. She wouldn't date and run as she'd done with other men.

Anika smoothed a hand over the silky skin of his chest and stroked the line of hair that covered his body, all the way down to where it descended below the waistband of his trousers. His muscles were a sight to behold. It wasn't enough to touch him. She showered kisses on his chest that made him push out a low groan and licked his nipples until they transformed into hard little nubs.

The rest of his clothes came off with a quickness, and then Reed's moist lips landed on her skin with a tender, almost reverential delivery before he shifted to stand on the side of the bed. He reached for her panties, and she lifted up so he could slide them down the length of her legs.

When she was completely naked, he lowered back onto the bed and braced himself above her. His gaze was like a soft caress, roaming over her bare shoulders and her swollen brown nipples tilted up to the ceiling. She ran her fingertips over her own sensitive flesh and watched his blue eyes darken to cobalt. Her nipples ached for his touch and fortunately, finally, became the focus of his undivided attention.

Reed ran his palms across the turgid peaks before closing one big hand over her right breast. He squeezed it. He massaged it. Until she sucked air through her teeth in pleasure-filled distress.

Then his mouth enveloped the nipple of the left breast. Moist and warm, his mouth was relentless. He teased the throbbing nub with his teeth and tortured it with his tongue. His avid attention elicited a shiver and a moan, and a choked sound of helplessness that caught in her throat. Reed took his time, alternating between delivering open-mouthed kisses to the soft mounds and tonguing her nipples.

"Reed, Reed," Anika panted.

Barely able to contain the building pressure in her loins, she clutched handfuls of hair and held his face to her chest, straining her aroused body up to his.

His fingers traced the line of her waist and over her bare hips, then moved lower to the strip of hair at her privates where his feather-light touch made her sensitive skin tremble.

"No," she whispered in a shaky voice.

"No? I don't think you mean that, princess."

She didn't mean it. Not when her legs fell apart and he rubbed her clit with gentle but firm strokes. Not when her toes curled and her heels pushed into the bed as she lifted into his touch.

He pulled her on top of him, fisting a hand in her hair this time and grabbing her ass with a rough hand.

Anika took full advantage of her position. She bit down on his hard shoulder and then covered the red mark with a soothing lick. She rained kisses across his throat and let her hands run free—free to explore the hardness of his biceps and the strength of his chest. She took pleasure in his manly form —the hair-roughened skin, the hard contours of his torso, and the power in his thick thighs. He was a big, powerful animal. Incredibly made and beautifully male.

Her hand clasped the pulsing-hard readiness of him and his jaw twitched as he groaned. When she took the engorged flesh between her lips, Reed dragged air into his lungs with a harsh, loud whoosh. The firm flesh filled her mouth—smooth and taut, hot and heavy.

It turned her on to watch him lose control—to watch him slowly unravel as he fought not to unravel.

"Not yet," he muttered, and flipped her onto her back, effectively taking back control. "You're trying to kill me," he said, his voice husky as he took gentle nips at her neck.

"*You're* trying to kill *me*," she whispered back. "I want you now, Reed." She wiggled beneath him and tilted her hips at just the right angle so the tip of shaft pressed at the entrance to her sex. Lifting her hips, she applied a little pressure, eliciting a helpless groan from the back of his throat.

"Now," he agreed, reaching for a condom in the night-stand. As soon as he had sheathed himself in protection, he nudged her thighs apart and lifted one leg over his forearm. Slipping in with ease, he gripped the bedsheets as his hard flesh filled her.

"Yessss." Anika gasped, sinking her short nails into his buttocks. She marveled at how he completely controlled her body. The way her legs fell open in utter surrender. She was different with him. A tigress in bed, and utterly wanton.

Her fingers slid over the rippling muscles of his shoulders and upper back as his hips moved with the same motion of an undulating wave between her thighs. His gaze lowered to her jostling breasts and he reached for one taut nipple again, plucking it into his mouth and laving the flesh with his tongue. He moved faster. Shallow plunges became deep dives, and she yielded to the power in each driving thrust.

Anika bucked beneath him, taking him further in a fast

and frantic rhythm. The rattling bed testified to the strength of their passion.

"You... feel... so... damn... good." Reed growled in her ear. It was a raw and masculine sound. One that spoke of his need and illustrated his hunger.

Anika wrapped her arms around his neck and abandoned herself to the pleasure. She couldn't get enough of him. Not his warm breath as it singed the side of her neck nor the way his body moved inside of hers.

She belonged to him, just as sure as if he'd tattooed his name on her spine. Completely. Each movement of their bodies confirming the truth—a truth she had tried to run from but failed miserably to escape.

They climaxed together, a tangle of sheets, limbs, and gasping cries. In the blinding rush of release, Anika squeezed her eyes shut and was certain she saw stars. The soul-shattering intensity of the moment was almost too much to bear. Reed muttered a litany of curse words as she gripped his solid back.

Anika's strangled cries faded into whimpers as she came down off her high and Reed collapsed on top of her. She twisted her head and pressed her cheek to his. Her fingers gently stroked the back of his neck where damp tendrils curled against his skin.

Staring up at the ceiling, a quick tremor ran through her at the enormity of the revelation that crossed her mind. This wasn't just sex. This wasn't simply an intense reaction to great sex. Their lovemaking was an experience unlike any she'd had with any other man.

She'd thought she'd made a mistake and equated sex with intimacy and passion with love. But that wasn't the case. Everything she'd felt for him in Venice was real—vivid, whole, and true.

Her heart clenched as she faced the hard truth. She was completely in love with Reed Stewart.

CHAPTER 18

*A*nika's eyes flew open.

A strange bed. A strange room. Alone.

Her pupils adjusted to the darkness and her memory came back.

Reed.

She moaned softly and stretched. Where was he?

The slightly ajar bedroom door indicated he was out in the hall. He was talking in a low voice. Quietly, she slipped from the bed and pulled on his shirt. Padding across the carpeted floor, she peered through the opening and saw Reed on the phone.

"Are you having a good time?" he whispered. He waited, head bowed, listening attentively. "I'm glad to hear you're having fun with your cousins." He listened again. "Yes, I miss you very much. I'm coming to get you tomorrow, okay? Oh, I don't have to rush?" He laughed softly. "You really are having a good time."

A few minutes passed as he listened to what Anika imagined must be quite a story about the day Brielle had. His only comments were the occasional "Mhmm," and "Oh really?"

Anika felt like an intruder on this intimate moment, but she couldn't walk away. Their bond was a joy to witness.

"All right, sweetheart. Give the phone back to cousin Ryan and go to bed. It's late. I love you, too. Yes, we can go to the park tomorrow, but you have to go to sleep now. I'll see you in the morning."

Anika scurried across the bedroom on tiptoe, tossed the shirt back on the floor, and slid under the covers.

When Reed returned to the room and eased onto the bed, she reached for him. "Everything okay?"

"Yeah. I was talking to Brielle for a bit. Did I wake you?"

"No, I was already awake."

Reed turned his face into her neck and flung one muscular arm across her waist. She closed her arms around him and welcomed the comfortable weight of his body as it rested half on top of hers. She was wide awake now and so was he. They lay there quietly, simply listening to each other breathe.

"Tell me something I don't know about you," Anika said.

"Something you don't know about me. Hmm…what do you want to know?" His warm breath brushed her collarbone.

She absentmindedly played with his soft hair. "Tell me about your dad. You never talk about him. What does he do?"

Reed laughed. "My father does whatever he wants. Right now he's in California housesitting for some rich businessman who travels all the time. He lives in the guy's guesthouse with a girlfriend younger than I am. He's got room and board, so he doesn't need anything else. He's always behaved the same way my entire life."

"You don't behave like that."

"I used to." Reed rolled onto his back and folded an arm beneath his head. He stared up at the ceiling. "I got tired of the insecurity of the life I'd lived with my father. That's why I majored in accounting. I wanted to do something that offered stability and permanence. Well, that's not completely true." He laughed again, this time in a self-deprecating manner. "I also sucked at everything else. I'm a terrible writer and can't spell for shit. My academic advisor steered me towards accounting."

Running a fingertip along his shoulder, Anika asked, "Did your father exhibit the same tendency to be irresponsible when your mother was alive?"

"Not as bad. My mother was the responsible one for sure, a nurse. She always held a job, but my dad was a dreamer. The occasional odd job was enough for him. I'm not sure what she saw in him, to be honest. He's so different from everyone else in his family. I think maybe he just hated farm life in Oklahoma and wanted to get away from the structure and demands he grew up under. My mom, on the other hand..." He paused, a frown developed on his face. "I think she wanted to punish her strict parents, and marrying my father was an act of rebellion."

"How'd she die?" Anna asked gently.

A muscle in his jaw moved. "An idiot shot up the hospital where she worked, killing her and two patients. She wasn't even supposed to be at work that day. She'd taken someone else's shift to make extra money." His voice had become devoid of emotion.

"I'm sorry." Anika rested her head on his shoulder, offering what little comfort she could. She smoothed her hand over his chest, gliding her fingers through the silky hairs sprinkled across his torso.

"Mmmm. That feels good, babe."

They were quiet for a while. The lull in the conversation allowed them to simply be—to just enjoy each other's company.

"What about you? Tell me about your family."

"Well, you know I have two older brothers who live out of

state. I miss them, but they have their own lives. My parents married young and my dad was old-fashioned. He was the no-wife-of-mine-is-going-to-work type of man, and in a perfect world he would have lived forever. But he didn't."

"How did he die?"

"Brain tumor. His deterioration was gradual, and he didn't tell us what was happening to him. That was my dad. He worried about us constantly but never took care of himself. He had episodes of slurred speech and dizzy spells before my mother finally caught on and convinced him to go to the doctor. That's when they discovered the tumor."

"Damn."

"We had a few lean years after he passed away. Except for a brief period before she married my father, my mother had never worked, so she had no skills and no job experience. After he died, she took whatever jobs she could, usually working as a maid cleaning other people's houses or watching the neighbors' kids, that kind of thing. We made it through with help from family. My brothers got jobs and contributed to the household, and so did I once my mom said it was okay. We still help her out, but a few years ago she got her cosmetology license." Anika smiled then, recalling how excited her mother had been to finally have a piece of paper that indicated she had a skill. And not only did she have a skill, she could now support herself on her own terms. "She works at a salon, which is the perfect job because if there's one thing my mother knows how to do, it's look good."

They both laughed.

"Like mother like daughter." Reed gave her a quick squeeze.

"To some degree. But she did instill in me the importance of being able to take care of myself." That's why buying into Davenport Design Studio was so important. It was a way to secure her future, especially if there was no husband down the line.

Anika snuggled closer to Reed. "It was awfully late for Brielle to be up, wasn't it? Did she think she heard monsters tonight?"

"No. She hasn't complained about monsters in weeks, to be honest. I think she just couldn't sleep because she wasn't in her own bed. She went into my cousins' room and told them she wanted to talk to me, so they called." He ran his fingertips across her shoulder blades. "We had a very interesting conversation about babies."

Anika grew still. "Babies?"

"She wants a baby brother. My other cousin's wife, Sophie, stopped by with their little boy."

"Kids love babies. What did you tell her?" A queasy sensation hovered at the top of her throat.

"I told her that wouldn't happen anytime soon. She wasn't happy, but I think I put her off for a while." She could hear the smile in his voice.

Don't do it. Don't ask.

"How many more do you want?" Anika asked.

"I haven't thought about it much, but I guess two more would be nice." His fingers stilled on her skin. "How many do you want?"

"I don't think about it."

"But you want kids?" Something in his voice caught her attention. There was an edge—not quite curiosity—more of concern.

And why wouldn't he be concerned. Society dictated that having children was the norm. The baby watch commenced as soon as a couple got married, and magazines were filled with celebrities and their baby bumps. The message was clear: having children was not only expected, it should be celebrated.

Now was the time to come clean, but Anika wanted to enjoy this moment a little bit longer. She dreaded the change in Reed's attitude toward her. It was coming.

Anika shut her eyes. She would tell him, but not right now. So she answered the question with her own brand of honesty.

"Yes. I would love to be a mother."

CHAPTER 19

"*H*ey cuz!" Anika called as she walked up the driveway of her cousin's house.

Veronica Taylor, nicknamed Ronnie, was her complete opposite. Ronnie was an auto mechanic and preferred comfortable shoes, no makeup, and had worn her hair in a low-maintenance natural style for years.

As she approached, Ronnie looked up from crouching over a tool box beside her pickup. "Hey! What's up?"

"I was in the neighborhood and thought I'd stop by."

"Oh really?" Ronnie said skeptically.

"Fine, I wanted some ribs. Did Uncle Ezekiel fire up the grill today?"

Ronnie's father often grilled on Sundays after church. Newly married, he lived next door with his wife of over a year.

"Sorry to disappoint you, but he and Loretta went on a weekend trip with the church."

"Again? I swear, those seniors get around, don't they?"

"Tell me about it. They're always gone. At least they're out there being active, not stuck at home letting old age keep them in a rocking chair collecting dust." Ronnie rummaged in her tool box.

"What are you working on?" Inspecting the area, Anika searched for a place to sit. Finding none, she leaned against the interior wall of the garage.

"You planning to help me?" Ronnie asked, dragging her toolbox to the left front tire.

"And get dirt and grease all over my clothes? Thanks for the offer, but I'll pass."

Ronnie smirked. "That's what I thought. I'm changing the oil." She removed the oil cap from under the hood.

"How are the salsa lessons coming?"

Ronnie's fiancé, Diego, was Cuban and she took salsa lessons twice a week to prepare for the wedding in a couple of weeks. Being a no-frills type of bride, Ronnie's ceremony was going to be a small affair with a small wedding party. As the maid of honor, Anika's most demanding moment had been helping Ronnie pick out a dress. At one point, her cousin had insisted on giving up, but Anika talked her into staying at the boutique, and after two hours, they found the perfect gown.

Ronnie grimaced. "I still suck even with the dance classes. I tried to convince Diego to let me out of it, but he said if he has to learn the electric slide, I have to learn salsa."

Anika giggled. "He has a point, Ronnie."

"Who's side are you on?"

"Yours, of course!"

"Uh-huh. I'm hanging in there, but don't expect much. So what's going on with you?" Ronnie lay on her back on a mechanic's creeper and slid under the jacked up car.

Anika stuck her hands in the pockets of her denim dress. "Things are interesting."

"Interesting how?"

"I'm dating."

"You're always dating." She could hear her cousin tinkering under the car with a wrench.

"This is different. It's a little more serious."

"When did that happen? Did you meet him online?"

"I should start from the beginning. Remember when I told you that I'd only had sex with Emerson and Adrian?"

"Yes."

"That might have been a little white lie."

Half a beat later, Ronnie rolled from under the car and their gazes met. "How much of a lie?" She stood and wiped her fingers on a paper towel and then tossed it into a small trash can.

"It's not too bad. It's just that when I said that, I was only talking about domestic sex—as in sex in the United States."

Ronnie's eyebrows floated higher. "Um, how many extra penises are we talking about, when you say you were only counting—"

"No, no. It's not what you think. I just had sex with one other guy besides those two."

"And you didn't count him because it wasn't domestic sex?" Ronnie placed a hand on her hip. "Because international sex isn't real?"

"Please don't make fun of me."

"Well then, I need a little bit of an explanation of why you didn't tell me about the international peen you indulged in. Was he Italian? French? Details!" Ronnie grinned.

"You're not going to believe this, but I barely knew him."

Ronnie let out an exaggerated gasp.

Anika glared at her.

"Okay, okay. Continue."

"He's American. We worked together in the campus dining hall at GSU but we barely spoke. Most of the time we never even had the same shifts. It's crazy, but I saw him in Venice seven years ago, the summer before senior year. I was standing outside my hotel, and there he was."

"I vaguely remember you telling me about a guy you ran into from school. You said you hung out with him a few times, and the two of you did some sightseeing together, that kind of thing. Is that who you hooked up with?"

She'd greatly downplayed Reed's role in her vacation. "That's him."

"I'm amazed you had sex with a man you barely knew. Miss My-goodies-are-a-treasure-and-not-for-everybody. My body is a temple. The same person who was appalled that I had sex with Diego on top of a car?"

"He wasn't your boyfriend at the time, and do you have to remind me of all that right now?"

"Yes, I do. Miss I-can't-have-sex-unless-there's-an-emotional-connection." Ronnie folded her arms and stared at Anika with an arched brow.

"I really can't have sex with a man unless there's an emotional connection."

"Are you saying you were emotionally connected to him? A man you barely knew?"

It did sound far-fetched, but the heat and passion that brought them together had been real. After spending all that time together, sleeping with him had been completely natural, an organic result of the many hours they spent in each other's company.

"I was in a place where I needed"—she swallowed—"re-assurance, I guess. That's around the time Emerson and I broke up, remember? I was at my low point." He had made her feel sexy and desirable. Her ex had called her broken. Reed had made her feel whole.

"Oh." That single word carried a lot of disdain. Ronnie had never liked Emerson, but Anika didn't completely blame him for his reaction to her confession. She should have told him early on she couldn't have children. Instead, she'd waited until a year into their relationship, when he was talking marriage, and he'd been brutally honest. He'd accused her of being *dis*honest and told her that she should have shared that information up front.

But she'd been afraid of that very reaction. Despite anticipating it, when he broke up with her, she was crushed. She'd wanted to beg and cry, but she'd foregone the begging and cried in private. Considering how torn apart she'd been by their break up, her strong reaction to Reed only weeks later had come as a surprise.

"I don't know how to explain it, but every single one of my reservations flew out the window. Being with him was…intense."

Ronnie's eyebrow arched higher and a slow smile crossed her features. "You're blushing. It must've been really good."

Anika placed her hands to her flaming cheeks. "Better than Emerson, and made me think long and hard about what I'd been missing."

"What's his name?"

"Reed."

"So how did you two find each other again?"

She explained how he hired her firm to redecorate his house, the weeks they spent in each other's company, and her closeness not only to him, but his daughter, as well. "We've been spending time together whenever we can, and I know he wants more. He said he wants me to meet his family here in Atlanta."

"And what do you want?"

"I'm excited but nervous." Anika gnawed the inside of her cheek, hesitant to voice her true desires. "I want more, too, and I want to meet his family." Just the mention of taking that next step made her heart flutter uneasily.

Ronnie shrugged. "So meet his family." Tilting her head, her eyes turned sympathetic. "There's a but in there somewhere, and I don't know why. You obviously like him a lot."

"A lot." Anika wasn't ready to voice that she'd fallen in love with him again. She'd thought long and hard about it the other day while soaking in the tub. She could barely control her emotions and the way her body reacted to him just by being in his presence.

"Maybe you should just have fun and not stress about where the relationship is going."

"It's not possible to just have fun with him, and I know he wants more than a hookup this time. I doubted his intentions before, but he's made them clear."

"So you're into him and he's into you. There's chemistry and you're reunited. What's the problem?"

"You know what the problem is. He's our age and has a daughter who wants a little brother. She's a precious little girl with a big smile, who likes to hold hands and cuddle and ask way too many questions." She laughed shakily and stared at her hands. "He wants more kids. Two more, he said." Anika bit her lip.

Ronnie flung an arm around Anika's neck, and Anika rested her head on her shoulder. One thing she couldn't complain about was lack of support. Her mother, brothers, and Ronnie had all been supportive and never treated her differently because of her medical situation. She was harder on herself than anyone else.

"You have to tell him," Ronnie said softly. "If you don't, you could end up in the same situation you did with Emerson. You don't want that, do you?"

"No," Anika said quietly.

At one point in time she had convinced herself that she no longer cared if she could be a mother or not. Children were messy and loud. Their little hands were often dirty or sticky from some mystery substance. But the sentiment hadn't lasted. All it took was spending a few hours with one of her brother's children, and the baby lust came back full blast, reminding her that she was a lone wolf. An oddity in society.

Why couldn't she be like her boss, Laura, and accept her

situation? Because Laura had chosen to be childfree, but the choice had been taken away from Anika.

"When do you see him again?" Ronnie asked.

"Next Sunday, when we go to his cousin's house."

"Can you see him before then?"

"Probably."

"Find a way to get him alone, away from his daughter and any other distractions. Have a heart to heart and tell him."

Anika swallowed, fear and worry pressing at the back of her throat. "You're right. I need to tell him."

But even as she said the words, she wasn't sure she could.

CHAPTER 20

*A*nika didn't have that heart to heart with Reed. She kept putting it off and putting it off, and the next thing she knew, it was Sunday afternoon and she was standing in his cousin's yard.

The Stewart men were a good-looking lot. She didn't know what they were eating up in Oklahoma, but it resulted in three very handsome men, all with dark hair and great physiques.

Reed was in what appeared to be an intense conversation with Ransom, the eldest and chef of a local restaurant. He was currently busy at the outdoor kitchen cooking up a meal for the entire crew gathered in his backyard. Earlier the men had played a game of flag football, with the children participating and getting in the way with their utter disregard for the rules. They threw themselves on the grass and rolled around, and eventually the rules were abandoned altogether. At some point Reed lifted Ryan's son, Ryker, in the air with the ball, and they called themselves the champs. An argument ensued. She still didn't know who had won the game and was pretty sure neither did anyone else.

The rest of the group consisted of Ransom's younger brother Ryan, in the process of blowing up an inflatable movie screen for the animated film they planned to show later. His youngest son, almost two, played with colorful plastic toys near his feet. Shawna, Ryan's wife, lounged in a chair on the lawn, dividing her attention between talking to her husband and watching her older son and daughter jump on the trampoline with Brielle.

"Hi, there. Welcome to our home." Sophie, Ransom's wife, approached Anika, who lingered at the refreshments table, sipping from a glass of lemonade.

Sophie had amber-toned skin and wore her thick hair in a loose bun on her head. "Sorry I couldn't meet you earlier, but I was on the phone and then had to feed my little guy."

"How old is your son?"

"Only a few months. I'm still getting used to being a mommy." She beamed.

"You must be exhausted," Anika said politely.

"He's a handful, and I am exhausted, but it's a good kind of exhausted."

Every mother said the same thing. No matter if they stayed up all night and struggled the next day from lack of sleep. No matter if there didn't seem to be enough minutes in the day to work, engage with their partner, and handle the burping, feeding, and changing of diapers. They all made it sound as if being exhausted and lacking time and energy was the best feeling ever.

Sophie poured herself a glass of tea and took a sip. "Mmm, this is good. Speaking of handfuls, Ransom told me about your experience with Brielle and how you saved Reed one day."

"Oh, it was nothing." She brushed away the praise.

"I wouldn't say that. I've never seen one of her tantrums, but I've heard they can be quite...energetic, and she's hard to handle in that state."

"Brielle is a sweet little girl and except for the tantrum, well-behaved," Anika said.

"Do you have kids of your own?"

It was a simple question and one that she'd been asked before. Anika usually had a quick, simple answer: No. But today of all days, being asked that amongst this close-knit family, with everyone playing and laughing together, the reality of her situation hit home.

At eighteen years old, she'd been in agony from cysts that had taken over her ovaries. Three different doctors came to the same conclusion: she needed to have her ovaries removed. So no, not only did she not have children, she never could.

She turned away from Sophie for a moment so the other woman couldn't see the pain that crossed her face. Tossing a crumpled napkin in the nearby trash, she said, "No kids for me."

"I don't blame you. There's no rush. Enjoy your freedom while you can." Sophie laughed. "I love my little bear, but life has certainly changed with him around."

"Come and get it!" Ransom called. He and Reed carried trays of grilled meat and sides from the kitchen. Screaming children scampered toward the wooden table and benches.

"*Bon appétit*," Sophie said.

Anika sat next to Ransom, while Ryan, Sophie, and Reed sat on the other side of the table, with Sophie in the middle. Shawna sat with the children at the other table, holding her youngest on her lap.

"So my loser cousin said you guys met back in college?" Ransom inclined his head at Reed and reached for a piece of bread, deliciously pungent with garlic butter soaked into it.

"I can hear you," Reed said.

"Honey, be nice," Sophie said to her husband.

Ransom grinned without remorse and bit into the bread.

"We worked at the dining hall on campus," Anika replied.

"And she couldn't keep her eyes off me," Reed added.

"Absolutely not true." Anika tossed a cherry tomato at him, which he caught and popped in his mouth.

"Consider yourself lucky that you didn't pay him any mind back then. He had quite a reputation," Ryan said.

"Oh, I know all about his reputation." Anika sipped her beer.

Reed folded his arms on the table and unabashedly stared at her. He had a way of looking at her as if no none else was present. "All of that is in the past. You're stuck with me now."

"Being stuck with you isn't so bad. I could think of worse things," Anika said.

"I told Reed he should have invited you over for a different occasion—a less chaotic meal without kids running around everywhere," Ransom said.

Sophie spoke up. "That would be misleading. Better she sees us in the midst of all the craziness so she knows up front what she's getting herself into."

"In that case, somebody pull her aside and warn her about Reed," Ryan said.

The men chuckled.

"Guys, you're going to scare her off." Sophie elbowed Ryan beside her. "Don't listen to them."

"Oh, I almost forgot. Anika's going to be signing some very important documents at the end of the week," Reed said.

"You're not supposed to talk about it! It might not go through. I don't want to get jinxed." Anika covered her face.

"You won't get jinxed."

"What? Tell us!" Sophie said.

"She won't brag on herself, so I'll brag on her." Reed reached across the table and held her hand. "At the end of the week, she's meeting with an attorney to sign documents that give her a stake in the design firm she works for, Davenport Design Studio."

"Oh, that's wonderful! Congratulations!" Sophie said.

Reed grinned at her across the table.

"Thank you," Anika mouthed to him. She was so lucky to have him in her life. Someone she could call a friend, a confidante, and a cheerleader.

"We have to celebrate. Toast!" Sophie hopped up from the table and held up her beer. "A big ole congratulations to you. Hopefully, we haven't scared you off. We want to have lots more celebrations with you."

"Here! Here!"

They clinked their beer bottles together, and tears pricked her eyes. She hadn't expected Reed's family to be so welcoming and friendly.

A loud scream came from the other table and cut through the celebration. Madison, Ryan and Shawna's daughter who was a little older than Brielle, held her arm aloft. "A spider! Mommy, get it off me! Get it off!"

Shawna had her hands full with her toddler and turned to her husband. "Ryan, could you please—"

He'd already set down his beer and was on his feet. "Ah, the joys of fatherhood," he said, rushing to the rescue.

They spent the rest of the afternoon in the same vein, alternating between teasing conversations and kid emergencies cropping up. Later, when they were all full and the children sprawled on old blankets on the grass watching a Disney movie on the blow-up screen, the adults seated behind them whispering together and holding hands, Anika thought what a beautiful scene this made. One she could well imagine playing out repeatedly over the years with an expanding brood. One that she wanted to be a part of.

The problem for her was, she didn't know how she could possibly fit in.

CHAPTER 21

*A*nika loved weddings.

The cake, the dress, and everything about the ritual of watching two people come together as one never got old. Standing beside her cousin as maid of honor only sweetened this particular ceremony. Ronnie had selected a plum-colored off-the-rack dress—an outfit Anika could see herself wearing again—for both of her bridesmaids. Flowers tucked above their right ear completed the ensemble.

Anika's favorite part of any wedding day, however, was the reception, when family and friends joined the bride and groom in the ultimate celebration before they left for their new life together. They were at that point now. The speeches were over, Ronnie had danced with her father and her husband and, in Anika's humble opinion, done an excellent job with the salsa.

"Hey." Ronnie hugged Anika around the waist from behind and rested her chin on her shoulder. "What are you doing over here in the corner?"

"Hiding," she answered honestly.

"Why?" Ronnie let go and stood next to her.

Anika had never seen her cousin look more lovely. Her

143

dark umber skin simply glowed, the perfect contrast to the white dress, whose off-the-shoulder sheer sleeves sparkled like the rest of the gown.

She regretted her answer when she saw the worry etched in her cousin's features. "Today is your wedding day and I don't want to spoil it."

"I'm way too high for you or anyone else to spoil my day. Tell me why you're hiding." When Anika didn't answer, she asked, "Is it Reed?"

"No, it's me." She chewed her upper lip, watching him over near the French doors, engrossed in conversation with her brother, Ian, who was in town for the wedding.

"What do you mean?" Ronnie asked.

"I think it's time for us to end our relationship. It's run its course." At least, that's what she'd told herself.

"You didn't tell him, did you?" Ronnie asked gently.

Anika swallowed. "No," she said quietly. She didn't know how. Date and run had been her modus operandi for years with men her age. It kept her heart safe and meant she could avoid a tough conversation. With other men it had been easy. With Reed, impossible. She loved him, and she couldn't come up with an easy way out.

"Forget about your fears and be honest. You'll never know his thoughts about your situation until you tell him."

Anika shook her head vehemently. "I can't. Then he won't want me anymore." Her voice shook. Voicing her fears made them more real.

"You don't know that."

She laughed humorlessly, her eyes scanning the gathered crowd. Everyone talking, eating, and drinking. Drunk on happiness and champagne.

"Did it ever occur to you that you're being unfair to him?"

Her mouth fell open. She'd never considered how he felt, too busy worried about her own insecurities and her own heart. "How?"

"He's investing time into this relationship. He deserves to know up front so he can decide if he can handle this situation. I think he can."

"I thought Emerson could, too." But Emerson had even said no to the idea of adoption.

Ronnie followed her gaze. "Reed's not Emerson, and Reed seems like a good guy."

"He is, but part of me wishes I hadn't gone down this road in the first place. Just continued as I was going, dating the men I was dating."

"So you want to keep offering yourself as a sacrifice to men twice your age?"

Anika bumped her cousin's arm with her elbow. "They're not that bad. I've met some good ones."

"More bad than good if I remember."

"*Hola*, my wife." Diego sauntered up, his green eyes filled with love.

Ronnie's face brightened, understandably so. Despite the dress shirt and slacks, Diego had a rugged sexiness about him, and that Cuban accent only added to his appeal. Right now he appeared ready to toss his bride over his shoulder and carry her away to be ravished.

"Your wife is trying to cheer me up. Please remind her that it's her wedding day and she needn't worry about me. She should be enjoying herself." Anika squeezed Ronnie in a one-armed hug. "Congratulations, you guys."

Before walking away, Ronnie caught her by the arm. "Think about what I said. Rip off the Band-Aid and get it over with."

"I'll think about it." The couple strolled away hand-in-hand, and Anika remained alone, silently observing Reed.

Ronnie was right. What she was doing wasn't fair to him. She knew he cared about her. Whenever he talked about future plans, he always included her, the assumption obvious that he expected her to be there. But she couldn't help but

145

think that asking him to accept her as is was asking too much.

Taking a deep breath, she walked over to where Reed was still engrossed in conversation with her brother. She linked an arm through his.

"What are you two talking about?" she asked, adding cheeriness to her voice.

"Nunya," Ian replied, reaching for her nose.

Anika slapped away his hand. "Would you cut it out? We're not kids anymore."

Ian smirked, unrepentant in his role as big brother and harasser. "A bunch of us are going to Dilligan's later to hang out. You guys coming?"

Reed shook his head regretfully. "Wish I could, but I need to leave soon." He scowled at his watch. "I've got a little one at home."

"Oh yeah? Girl or boy?" Ian asked.

"Girl. Four and a half years old."

"I've got three. My boy is six and the girls are seven and ten." Ian was a doting papa. Anika was surprised he didn't whip out his wallet and show off his kids.

"I'd like to have two more myself, and get at least one boy in there." Reed smiled down at Anika.

Heat crawled up her neck.

"Oh. Really?" A strange expression came over Ian's face. The heat rose into Anika's cheeks, but she returned her brother's gaze without flinching.

Reed slipped his arm around Anika's waist, keeping her close to his side. She leaned into him, the support of his solid body adding much-needed comfort.

"My family teases me that I'll probably end up with all girls. Karma for past behavior." Reed chuckled. "But honestly, I don't care if I have two more girls, as long as my kids are healthy."

Ian nodded. "I hear you." He cleared his throat, glanced at

Anika, and then directed his conversation to Reed. "Kids are definitely a blessing, but I think even more important is finding someone you can spend the rest of your life with. You know, someone you can share the ups and downs with. Someone you can count on. That's not always easy to find."

"No, it's not. But when you find that person, it's best to hold on to them."

"Exactly. No matter what." A self-satisfied smile crossed Ian's face, as if what he'd said accomplished something.

"Thank goodness we don't have to choose. We can have both. That special someone *and* a family."

Reed squeezed her waist, and Anika offered him a weak smile. She didn't need any more signs to let her know that Reed should be told the truth.

"Yeah." Ian cleared his throat again. "My wife is motioning me over there, not too subtly. Looks like she wants me to meet someone. It was nice talking to you, Reed. Anika, give me a call later or tomorrow when you're free. I'd like to catch up." He sent a meaningful glance her way and headed across the dance floor.

"Your brother's a cool guy," Reed said. "Except for when he asked about my intentions toward you."

Anika's eyes widened. "Please tell me you're kidding."

He chuckled, his eyes lighting up in the most beautiful way. "I am kidding. He didn't ask me that."

"Thank goodness." Anika breathed a sigh of relief, though she wouldn't put it past her brother to do that and think it was hilarious. "To be honest, though, I would have been surprised. Ian is more laid back than my other brother. He'd have to catch you kicking a puppy to dislike you."

"So you don't think it's my charming personality that won him over?"

"Oh, I'm sure that helped."

Reed rubbed his hand up and down her back, his lids

lowering and his voice dropping an octave. "You coming by later?"

She wanted to. She really, really wanted to, but didn't think she could handle being in his presence alone. She felt extremely fragile and had a lot to think about, not the least of which was figuring out how to broach the subject of her infertility.

"No. I'm going to stick around here and help with cleanup, and then I'm going home. It's been a long day and I just want to crash."

"Crash at my place." He swept his gaze over her body as if he wanted to strip her naked right then and there. The blatant hunger in his eyes made her skin tingle all over. "I'll sneak you up to my bedroom, and you can stay the night. Leave early in the morning."

They had decided not to let Brielle see her spend the night at his place yet.

"What if Brielle comes in during the night?"

"She's been fine for weeks. No talk about monsters in a long time."

Anika slipped out of the cradle of his arm. "That's a tempting offer, but I want to sleep in my own bed tonight."

The smile slowly faded from his face. "Is everything okay?"

"Yes. Why?"

"I don't know. You've just been acting strange lately. Ever since we had dinner at Ransom and Sophie's. Did someone in my family say something to upset you?"

"Not at all. Every single one of them was very friendly." They'd welcomed her without any discernible reservations.

"You sure?"

"Positive." His misplaced concern twisted guilt into her gut. He was being so considerate, worried about her needs and happiness. She should do the same for him. Show the same consideration for his needs. His happiness.

"Would you tell me if someone said something to upset you?"

"I would," she assured him.

He seemed satisfied with the answer. "On that note, I better leave." He took her hand in his. "Call me when you get done here."

"I will."

They kissed, but when he went to pull back, Anika gripped his arm in an act of desperation. She held on tight, keeping her mouth pressed to his and forcing a deeper kiss.

When Reed finally lifted his head, he frowned down at her. "Anika—"

"Go. Don't keep Mrs. Miller waiting."

He hesitated. A mixture of confusion and concern filled his eyes, but he seemed to think better of questioning her further. "We'll talk later."

He squeezed her hand and walked away.

CHAPTER 22

$\mathcal{R}$eed lounged on the sofa in the living room, bare feet propped on the ottoman. He stared at the painting he bought during the art stroll. Anika had been radiant that night, with her curly hair and that damn dress with the plunging neckline that fit to all her curves. She'd been a walking temptation.

Reed rubbed his jaw. Brielle was fast asleep upstairs, and for the umpteenth time he checked to make sure the landline had a dial tone and his cell phone wasn't on silent mode. Anika hadn't called yet, and it was getting late. If her behavior over the past week was any indication, she probably wouldn't call. He couldn't put his finger on the exact problem, but he'd noticed a change in her attitude. She'd become withdrawn. Their normal two-hour conversations had whittled down to fifteen minutes, and they conversed more like acquaintances than lovers.

Brielle missed her, too. This morning over a bowl of Cheerios she'd asked when Miss Anika would be coming to visit. He'd mumbled something vague because he didn't have a real answer.

He'd never been more certain of the closeness between

Anika and Brielle than when he found them both asleep on the sofa one night. Anika lay in a protective curl around his daughter, near the edge, with Brielle tucked safely on the inside against the back of the chair. He'd lost track of how long he stared at the two of them in that position.

Despite what Anika said, he called Ransom and Ryan tonight, asking if they or their wives had said something to upset her. Neither could shed any light on the change he observed. As far as they were concerned, she'd been the perfect guest, and there had been no conflict.

His doorbell rang and Reed's gaze went to the clock on the fireplace mantle. It was almost eleven o'clock. Shuffling to the door, he peered out and saw Anika standing on the porch. He swung open the door, ridiculously happy to see her. She must have changed her mind, and all the concern he'd had drifted away.

She still wore the plum-colored halter dress, the deep hue enhancing her golden brown skin.

"Hey beautiful, get in here." He reached for her, but she stepped back.

"I should have called first, but I couldn't. I've been looking everywhere for my phone, and then I remembered I gave it to you at the wedding venue."

That's right. She'd asked him to hold her phone because she wanted to leave her purse locked in the car.

"I completely forgot. It's still in my jacket pocket. I'll get it for you." He stepped aside so she come in, but she didn't move.

"Aren't you going to come in?"

"I can't. I've got to run."

"Run where?"

"Home. Could you just get the phone for me?"

What the hell?

"Sure. Give me a sec."

Reed ran up the stairs and found the phone in his jacket, which he'd thrown across the foot of the bed.

Back downstairs, he handed it over to Anika.

"Thanks. Have a good night." She turned away.

"That's it?"

She paused, her brow wrinkling. "I told you I couldn't stay."

A tight knot of apprehension filled his chest. "What is going on with you? We need to talk."

"There's nothing for us to talk about. I have a lot on my mind right now."

"And you can't share that with me?"

"It's not something I can share at the moment," she said testily.

"Why the hell not? Isn't that what couples do? Share the good and the bad? Something is wrong and you won't tell me what it is."

"Reed, please. Don't do this."

"Don't do what?"

"Push."

"You realize you're talking to the wrong guy, right?"

Her face transformed before him, from angry to weary. "You want to know what's wrong? You want to talk? Fine. This relationship isn't working for me."

"Bullshit. You've been happy. What's wrong?" Reed remained in the same spot and folded his arms across his chest.

"What do you want me to say?"

"Tell me the truth. Don't hit me in the gut with some nonsense about our relationship not working for you. Since when? I just met your mom and the rest of your family at your cousin's wedding. A week ago I introduced you to my family."

"I never asked you to introduce me to your family."

"So does that mean you don't want to be a part of my life?

You don't want to be a part of Brielle's life? Because if that's the case, then you need to let me know right now. It's one thing to play with my emotions, but I won't let you play with my daughter's."

Her eyes widened. "Don't accuse me of playing games with her emotions or yours. That's not fair."

"Then what the hell is going on right now?" His voice had gotten louder, more panicked. "Is this just a fucking game where you mess with my head and rip my heart out? Are you punishing me for what I did seven years ago?"

"No!"

"Then why? Why are you saying our relationship isn't working for you? I love you! What am I supposed to do with that?"

Reed froze. The shock of his words blindsided him. Her, too, apparently. Her mouth fell open. He hadn't meant to admit his love for her in such a raw fashion, but the words were out there now. A scary and unfamiliar sensation beat his chest. He was wide open, his soul laid bare to her.

"Should I act as if the past couple of months didn't mean anything?" he asked in a quieter tone.

"That's not what I said," she whispered, sounding defeated.

"Help me to understand, Anika."

"You're so perfect, Reed. You're considerate and thought-ful. You're a good father." Her shoulders drooped. "Being with you is so hard," she said in a low tone.

"It doesn't have to be. If I'm doing something wrong, tell me."

She stared at the wooden slats in the porch.

"Come inside so we can talk."

"No."

"Why not?"

"If I come inside, I'll change my mind about what I have to do."

He didn't like the sound of that at all. "If you're afraid you'll change your mind, then you aren't really sure about your decision." When she didn't respond, he continued. "I don't want to lose you. You're important to me. I love you."

She lifted her gaze. "How long do you think your love will last?"

He was in the fight of his life. He was definitely losing her.

"I don't see my love diminishing in the least. It hasn't in seven years. I knew in Venice that you were the woman for me, but I was too chicken to do anything about it. I was dumb and young and thought I wanted to sow my wild oats instead. Had I been smart, I would've taken you up on your offer to stay in touch."

She hugged herself and blinked away tears. "Everything you say is what I've wanted to hear. I want to believe you."

Her sadness tore up his soul. He wanted to ease the hurt and pain so evident in the depths of her eyes.

"These aren't only words. I'm speaking the truth. My truth. The truth of a grown, mature man who has learned what's really important in life. It took me a while to figure things out, but I have. Whatever's wrong, we can work through it."

"How can you be certain that you love me, and how can you be sure that it will last?"

"Because I've never felt like this before," Reed said, his voice earnest and hoarse. "I know that my love will last because my feelings are so deep and so wide for you that there's literally no end in sight." He cupped her face in one of his hands. "I know because it feels right, and has felt right since the beginning. Since Venice, when it felt like we were hidden away from the rest of the world, just the two of us for a little while, for that brief moment in time. I forgot every-thing and everyone, and the same forgetfulness overcomes me every time we're together. I've never experienced that with anyone else, and I want to feel that way forever."

He bent his head and kissed her, testing her soft lips and savoring the softness of her mouth against his. He never grew tired of kissing Anika. She really was the perfect temptation, a little bit sweet but with the right amount of sexiness to keep him interested.

"Tell me what I did to make you want to run from me."

"You didn't do anything. I simply had to face reality." Tears shimmered in her eyes.

"What reality?"

"That I can't give you what you want."

"What do you think I want?" He laughed, but panic clotted in his chest.

"Something important. I know that if I can't give it to you, you'll stop wanting me."

"I'll never stop wanting you."

"I wish I could believe you."

"How bad could it be?"

"Really bad." She covered her face with her hands. "Oh god, I'm not ready to do this." She breathed the words in a broken whisper.

"Anika, talk to me. What is it?"

She took a deep breath. "I can never have kids." She studied his face, anxious to read his expression.

Reed blinked. "What do you mean—"

"I mean, I can*not* have children. I'll never get pregnant."

Then he did the same thing she'd seen many times before: his gaze dropped to her stomach. "Ever?"

His doubt wrenched through her gut. "Ever."

"There must be something. Medicine has come a long way. There are plenty of people who think they could never have children who do, thanks to fertility treatments. There *are* options."

"There are no options for me. There's no magic pill that can fix me."

"How can you be so sure?"

Anika licked her lips. "When I was eighteen, I had to have my ovaries removed. That's what caused the small scars on my stomach. I was in a lot of pain, and after talking to multiple doctors, I made the difficult decision to have them removed."

Reed ran his hand through his hair. "Help me out here, because it's been a while since I've had biology, but the ovaries are where the eggs are made?"

"That's right. Both of mine are gone, so I can't produce any more eggs."

"S-so…" He frowned.

"I can never have kids, Reed. That's why we can't be together."

His eyes widened. "Wait a minute, you're moving too fast. Who said we can't be together? Give me a minute to digest all of this."

"There's no need." She already knew what was coming and took off toward the car, moving on quick feet.

"Where are you going?" She was down the steps before he caught her by the arm. "Anika."

"Stop it!" She jerked away and hurried forward.

He grabbed her by the arm again and swung her around to face him. "Goddammit, we're not done talking!"

Anika tugged away. "Don't pretend it doesn't matter because I can see it in your face."

"I'm in shock. I've seen you with my daughter. I assumed…" His voice trailed off as he parsed his words, trying hard not to hurt her or make a verbal faux pas.

"And I've seen you with your daughter." Her voice came stronger. "And your little cousins. And listened to you talk about having siblings for Brielle. If you and I were together, I couldn't give either of you that."

She marched toward the car again.

"Stop moving!"

She faced him, anger boiling up inside of her. This was so

156

unfair. Why did he have to come back into her life? Why couldn't he just leave her alone?

"Why? What are you going to say? That we'll get through it and it doesn't matter? For how long? How long before you regret your decision, resent me, and wish that my infertility wasn't true? Before you long for another baby—your own blood?"

He ran his fingers through his hair. "Yes, I said I want more kids, but you're being very unfair and making assumptions about my thoughts and my wishes."

"I'm not wrong. But I don't blame you, Reed. Believe me, I understand. You wanted to know why Emerson broke up with me, and this is why. I don't expect you to be any different. I want you to have that little girl and little boy you so desperately want. I'm just not the woman to give them to you. I'm messed up. I'm b-broken, and there's no miracle drug in the works for me. I won't magically get pregnant. It can't happen. It won't happen. Ever." Her voice cracked.

"Sweetheart."

He stepped toward her, but she pulled back as if he were a leper.

"Don't." She drew a trembling breath. "It's better this way. Trust me. Two years from now, I don't want you to long for more or think I'm not enough—that I wasn't worth the sacrifice."

"I would never think that. You're everything to me."

"Good night, Reed."

"Anika, wait." His voice was hoarse, his face tortured, but she knew it would pass.

She quickly slipped into the car and locked the door.

"Anika, wait! Don't drive off."

She started the vehicle.

Reed pounded on the window so hard she worried he'd smash the glass. Ignoring him, she concentrated on backing out and getting as far away as possible.

"Open the door. Open the door. We're not done talking!" Jogging along beside the car, he yanked the handle. "Anika!"

Next door, a light came on in the first floor of his neighbor's house.

Anika continued backing toward the street.

"Open the door! Don't drive away from me. Don't drive away!"

She reversed faster, and he ran after her, but she pulled out into the street. He stood at the end of the driveway, breathing heavily. He looked back at the house and then at her, his eyes begging her to stop. He couldn't leave. Not with Brielle upstairs. She drove off, the sound of his yells muffled by the distance and rolled up windows.

She pounded the steering wheel as tears filled her eyes. "Shit, shit, shit."

She wished a lot of things. She wished Judge Evers had never recommended her firm to Reed. She wished he'd never walked through their doors. She wished she hadn't been assigned to his project.

But more than anything, she wished she hadn't fallen in love with him and fooled herself into having hope. Because now she had to spend the rest of her life knowing what she was missing.

CHAPTER 23

"*I* don't want to talk to Grandma," Brielle said quietly. She sat on the sofa in the den, hands clasped on her lap, body slumped into a miserable little curve.

"Why not?"

Reed crouched before her. He was tired. He hadn't slept a wink last night for thinking about Anika. Then bright and early this morning, Nanette called to blast him for not letting her speak to her granddaughter.

Brielle used to love talking to her grandmother and had even memorized the Dallas number so she could call herself. He wanted them to stay in touch, recognizing that her grandmother was a connection to not only her maternal history, but her African-American heritage.

"I get sad when I talk to her," Brielle murmured.

Reed took her hands in his and rubbed his thumb along her little fingers. "I know it makes you sad, but grandma loves you. She wants to talk to you for a few minutes, and you haven't talked to her in a very long time. She misses you. Don't you miss her?"

Brielle nodded, and he wasn't sure if she was telling the truth or if she'd simply nodded to appease him.

He couldn't put off Nanette any longer. For a whole month Brielle had said she didn't want to talk to her, and he'd allowed it. But her grandmother was furious and accused him of not only keeping them apart, but alienating her from her grandbaby. He'd permitted Brielle to dictate whether or not she talked to her grandmother, but that was wrong. A four-year-old child should not make that kind of decision—especially when it meant losing touch with family who loved her.

"Tell you what, spend a few minutes on the phone. I'll be nearby—right here in the kitchen where you can see me—and when you get off the phone, if you're sad, we'll talk about it. Okay?"

She nodded again but didn't make eye contact.

"That's my girl." Reed kissed her knuckles and lifted to his feet. "Here's the phone. You remember the number?"

Brielle nodded and took the cordless. When she started dialing, he went into the kitchen. From there, he had a clear view to the den because of the modifications made by the design team.

He kept busy making iced tea. Pulling the ingredients from the cabinets, he thought about Anika. What was she doing now?

Reed measured the ingredients into a glass pitcher. As he worked, he glanced up to see how Brielle was doing.

He'd learned to stop hovering while she talked to her grandmother. The therapist had said to give her space and let her breathe, which hadn't been easy to do. As her sole parent, he'd been overprotective in the new role of father and mother, but he'd always obliged.

As he stirred the iced tea, he watched his daughter, the phone up to her ear, head and shoulders still bent in a sign of...what?

He stopped stirring and really paid attention to her body language. She'd been so excited earlier today when they'd gone to the park. There'd been a sparkle in her brown eyes. Laughter on her lips. The simple, pure joy of childhood as she ran and climbed throughout the playground with the other kids.

But now, Brielle looked...defeated. She kept her eyes downcast and her gaze planted on some spot on her lap.

Something wasn't right. She seemed to have a full-on aversion to talking to her grandmother.

With a knotted stomach, Reed eased the extension from its cradle. He listened to Nanette speaking in her grandmotherly voice.

"...and don't you want to come back to Dallas, to be with Grandma? Grandma misses you, and so does Pop Pop. We all miss you, but your daddy's not going to let you come back. You've got to show him that you're not happy. You've got to—"

"What are you doing?"

Reed's voice cracked with the force of a firecracker through the line. He could hardly breathe. His gaze rested on Brielle, and she lifted her head. The look in her eyes—the sadness—tore at him. She shouldn't know sadness or have to concern herself with pleasing anyone. Her only concern should be which stuffed animal was going to suffer through her choke hold later tonight.

"I said, what are you doing?" he demanded in an even louder voice. Silence greeted the question. "Hang up the phone, Brielle. Right now." Brielle just stared. "I said hang up the phone."

She hung up. Her lower lip trembled and her face crumbled.

Reed muted the phone. "Go to your room, sweetheart. You're not in trouble. Go upstairs, and I'll be there in a few minutes."

Brielle ran off. He listened to her footsteps hurry down the hallway and climb the stairs.

Reed unmuted the phone. "Care to tell me what the hell you think you're doing? Is this what your conversations have been about all along? You've been turning my daughter against me?" He'd had his suspicions but hadn't wanted to believe the worst of Nanette, quickly and guiltily casting aside his negative thoughts.

"I haven't been turning her against you." The grandmotherly tone was gone, and all that remained was cool disdain.

"Then what do you call what I just heard? You told her—"

"I don't know what you think you heard, but I was telling my granddaughter how much we miss her."

"And coaching her on how to throw tantrums and be disruptive?"

"I was not!"

"Don't deny it! Now everything makes sense. Every time she gets off the phone with you she's completely different. Then the next day she throws a goddamn tantrum, and now I know why."

"Watch your language with me, young man."

"Save me the respect-your-elders bullshit, Nanette. You've been creating problems for me on purpose. Why? Because you don't think I'm good enough to raise your granddaughter? Because you think you could do a better job?"

"A pack of wolves could do a better job," Nanette seethed, disgust dripping from her voice.

He'd suspected Nanette didn't care for him, but the disgust coming through the phone line—the utter vitriol that dripped from her voice had unmasked the true depth of her contempt.

"Brielle is mine. *My* flesh and blood, and I am going to raise her here, in Atlanta. I don't give a damn if you like it or not."

Nanette laughed. "Oh, I know. You don't give a damn about anything, do you? You never have."

"That is not true."

"After my daughter died, you swooped in here on your white horse to save the day, as if you had a clue how to raise that child."

"You've had a problem with me from the beginning. I'm sorry I'm not what you wanted, but *I am her father*, and I have a right to raise my daughter the way I see fit. And I see fit to raise her in Atlanta, with my family."

"You see fit?" Nanette's laughter came out as a derisive cackle this time. It lasted so long, Reed wondered if she'd ever stop. "You're right. I never wanted you anywhere near my daughter. But you see, I didn't have a choice. I thought Layla was making a mistake when she dated you. I knew it the minute I met you. I know your type. The irresponsible manwhore, only out for a good time. And I was right! You took advantage of her. You got her pregnant and then you disappeared."

"That's not what happened." He and Layla had had an understanding. They lived in different cities and were pursuing their individual career paths. A long distance relationship was perfect.

"I was the one who had to watch my daughter crying over a man who didn't deserve her tears."

Reed winced guiltily and ran rough fingers through his hair. "I cared about Layla."

"You cared about yourself. Where were you when she went into labor?"

"I was in New York. You know that."

"You should have been here! You knew when her delivery date was, and she was in delivery for ten hours."

"I had to catch a flight." He'd hopped on the first plane he could.

"I held her hand in the delivery room, and you showed up

two hours late. And two days later, you were gone. I helped raise that baby. For four years—four years we seldom saw you. You weren't her father. You were a stranger. The only thing you did consistently was send a check. I helped Layla raised that little girl. I stayed up nights so she could get some rest, and when she went back to work, Brielle stayed with me. *Every day.* I was her momma. I was her daddy. I was her nanny. I was her best friend. And then Layla died, and all of a sudden you want to be a full-time daddy? And you came, and you took my little girl." Tears thickened her voice now. "She's all I have left of my Layla, and you took her away from us. From me." Her voice cracked, and she was openly weeping now. "I can't see her anymore. I'm the stranger. She's all I have left of my daughter. My one and only. And you took her. You just took her!"

Reed closed his eyes. The sorrow in Nanette's voice ripped him apart and drained him of anger. She was still grieving the loss of her daughter and, in her own way, trying to hold on to the child she loved as her own.

He'd stepped up to be responsible and give his daughter love, and the security that he believed she needed from him. He'd wanted to be a better father than his had been. Yet he'd inflicted deep hurt on Brielle's family—an unintended consequence of trying to be a good man.

"Nanette, I'm sorry Layla's gone, and I'm sorry that you had to suffer the loss of your only child."

She sniffled.

"But what you've been doing is wrong. You're hurting Brielle and confusing her. I'm not going to give you any details about my relationship with Layla. That was private and between us, but I can assure you that I cared about her deeply."

Nanette must have started influencing Brielle's behavior after he bought the house. She recognized that he was not giving up and was setting down roots. He had no doubt she'd also unintentionally created the fear of monsters in Brielle. His daughter's anxiety over the conversations had manifested into monsters in the closet and under the bed.

"I admit, I wasn't the best father at first, but I love Brielle with all my heart. She changed me. I'm different because of her. I'm trying my damndest to be a good dad, and I'm getting there. Because of her, I'm a better person. I don't want to keep you two apart. She loves you, but what you're doing is hurting her so much that I had to convince her to call you. She didn't want to."

"What?"

"She's torn. She's hurting because you're making her choose sides. A four-year-old shouldn't be placed in that situation."

Nanette sniffled again, but didn't speak.

"I want you in her life. It doesn't have to be all or nothing for either of us. We can work this out."

She started crying again. He heard jagged huffs of breath as she fought to control her emotions.

"Can we try to work this out? For Brielle's sake?"

Nanette sniffed. "Yes. I'm willing."

Progress.

"I'm going to hang up and check on Brielle. I'll call you tomorrow and we can discuss some ideas. Maybe she can come stay with you part of the summer."

"Yes, yes. I'd like that," Nanette said quickly. "I still have a room in the house just for her."

"Okay. And um…maybe we could do FaceTime or Skype on the computer."

"My goodness, I don't know anything about that technology business. It's all so complicated."

"We'll figure it out. I promise you. If it means you can see Brielle more often, will you try?"

"You know I'd do anything for that child."

"I know. And thank you. Thank you for everything you've

done for Brielle, helping Layla, and in essence, for helping me."

"That's my baby." Her voice wobbled again, but she took a deep breath and gathered strength. "I'll let you tend to Brielle now. Make sure you tell her Grandma loves her to death, and she never ever has to hesitate to talk to me again. You make sure you tell her, you hear me?"

"I will. I promise."

"Good. We'll talk tomorrow then?"

"We'll talk tomorrow." Reed hung up the phone and ran a hand down his face. He expelled a breath of air and braced both hands on the granite bar top.

Now the mystery of Brielle's behavior had been resolved once and for all, he could concentrate on other things— namely, Anika. She'd referred to herself as broken. He winced. Had she carried around that thought all along? He'd have to find a way to convince her that his love was not conditional, and he wanted her just the way she was.

With that thought in mind, Reed headed upstairs to tend to his daughter.

CHAPTER 24

*T*oday was an exceptional day. Surrounded by her coworkers in the break room, Anika celebrated a professional milestone. She now owned a minor stake in Davenport Design Studio, giving her the right to participate in decision-making and share in profits. This also garnered her a new role as a senior designer, working strictly with the firm's high-end clients.

The fact that Laura had relinquished part of her company was nothing short of a miracle. She'd built the design firm from the ground up, but even more surprising, Anika learned during one of their private meetings that Laura intended to sell her a larger share of the company as time went on, if she was interested. She was definitely interested.

Laura stood at the front of the room and smiled at Anika with affection in her eyes. "I can't say enough how much I appreciate your dedication to this firm. You've shown it every day through your hard work, and our clients can't stop singing your praises. From the day I hired you, I knew you'd do great things, and you far exceeded my expectations. Now we get to be partners, and I can't wait to see what the future holds."

"Thank you for believing in me and giving me the opportunity," Anika said.

"Cheers!" the staff yelled, lifting glasses of champagne in the air.

Anika struggled to get into a cheery mood. Four days had passed since her confrontation with Reed, and not once had he called or come by her house. Now his absence confirmed what she'd feared—that his love was conditional. That he couldn't really love her the way she wanted—the way she needed. Just as she was.

She did her best not to think about him. The memories were too painful. She missed him too much—their closeness, their compatibility. They'd shared so many intimate moments —laughing at silly jokes, holding hands, cuddling.

Even worse, she didn't only miss him. She missed Brielle, too, with her giggles, the way she organized her stuffed animals, and the guileless trust in her brown eyes. If she could have a daughter, she'd want her to have Brielle's personality.

Anika sipped champagne from her flute and mustered a grin, even as the painful truth twisted inside her. "Okay, time for the sweet stuff." She cut into the cake, covered in buttercream frosting and *Congratulations Anika* written in red letters. This was only the first part of the celebration. The staff planned to meet for dinner and drinks after work. She wished she could get out of it, but as the guest of honor, that was impossible.

"Well, hello there."

Laura spoke in an unnaturally high-pitched voice, and Anika turned away from her conversation with Edgar to see Reed and Brielle standing inside the room.

Reed wore a black shirt and black pants. A fine growth of hair covered the lower part of his face. She hadn't heard from him in days, and then he shows up looking so good. Dark, brooding, and yummy.

Brielle was adorable with her hair parted in the middle and styled into Minnie Mouse buns. She vaguely wondered if Reed or Mrs. Miller had done her hair.

"Hi, Laura. I came to talk to Anika." His eyes never left Anika's face.

"Is everything okay?" Laura asked in the same odd-sounding voice. "Is there something we can help you with?" Laura was an excellent businesswoman and visionary when it came to design, but she was a terrible actress. She'd obviously been expecting Reed.

Anika set down her plate and glass with shaky hands. "We can go to my office," she offered. She did not want a public display of whatever Reed had planned.

He shook his head and walked farther into the room, his little sidekick coming along with him, clutching her denim jacket closed over a lavender T-shirt. "We need to talk, but what I have to say needs to be said in front of your coworkers."

Seized by panic, Anika shook her head vehemently. No way she wanted her dirty laundry to play out in front of the staff, and she couldn't believe Reed would put her in such a position. "Please let's go to my office. This is not the place and certainly not the time for whatever you have planned."

"Here and now is the perfect time and place to make a public declaration of my love for you."

Someone in the back gasped. Quiet descended on the room, and Anika held her breath. Bewildered, she could only stare at Reed, heart hammering at a violent speed.

He stepped closer and spoke in an even, quiet tone. "I messed up seven years ago when I walked out of your life. I thought it was the right decision, but I was wrong. Biggest mistake I've ever made. I'd lived most of my life not having any responsibility or concern for anyone or the future. I couldn't accept how much you meant to me until it was too late."

Anika's heart raced even faster, but she remained very still as she listened to him.

"We want the same things. We're more similar than we are different. I know you love me, and I love you. I loved you then and I love you now. To prove that, Brielle has something to show you."

Brielle stepped up, her cheeks bright with color, her brown eyes glowing with excitement. She opened her jacket and Anika's eyes landed on the gold letters written on the lavender T-shirt: *Please say yes.*

Reed lowered to one knee and held open a red box with a diamond solitaire sparkling inside. Gasps and a series of ahhs filled the room.

Anika's hands flew to her mouth. "What are you doing? What are you doing, Reed?" She wanted to cry and laugh at the same time. This couldn't be happening. Not to her.

"Proving to you that you're all I need. Just you. There's no sacrifice in being with you, sweetheart. The only sacrifice would be if I lost you." The sincerity in his eyes tightened the hold on her heart. "Anika, will you marry me? Please."

Choked with emotion, Anika remained frozen in place. She couldn't speak. She couldn't move. This was it. Reed wanted and loved her—Anika. She was enough. She wasn't broken. She was whole in her current form.

"Are you sure, because—"

"I'm sure." He meant it. She could see it in his eyes. "And I need an answer quickly because my knee is starting to hurt." He grinned.

Her face crumbled as she nodded. "In that case, yes, I'll marry you."

Her coworkers erupted into cheers, and Anika rushed over to Reed, cupping his face and kissing him hard on the mouth. He rose to his feet with his arms around her thighs and lifted her in the air, devouring her lips in a sweet, sultry kiss that made their audience cheer even louder.

Happiness swelled in her chest. "God, I love you," she whispered. "You knew, didn't you? How did you guess that I loved you?"

"It was obvious it hurt you to leave me, but you did it anyway because you thought that was best for me." The corners of his blue eyes crinkled as he smiled. "And because you never said you didn't."

She kissed him again to loud applause as Brielle danced around them, chanting repeatedly, "She said yes. She said yes."

EPILOGUE

*W*hen Anika finished brushing her teeth, she pulled her hair into a bun and padded back into the bedroom. Climbing into bed, she resumed reading the Agatha Christie novel she'd started the night before.

Today she was allowed to be lazy and was going to take full advantage. Later she'd go downstairs in her pajamas, but for now enjoyed the peace and quiet.

She was deeply engrossed in the book when a knock at the door disrupted her concentration. "Come in."

In came her husband and children.

First up was Brielle, prancing into the room dressed in princess pajamas and her hair full and bountiful around her shoulders. She was followed by her 18-month-old brother, Jaden. Anika and Reed adopted him less than a year ago. Reed pulled up the rear carrying a bed tray of breakfast food.

"Happy Mother's Day!" Brielle and Reed yelled.

Jaden repeated something that came out more garbled but sounded similar. With his toasty brown skin and dimpled smile, he looked simply ecstatic to be a part of the surprise, even if he didn't fully comprehend what was taking place.

"What is all this?" Anika asked. She was genuinely

surprised. She and Reed had agreed her gift would be spending the day in solitude with no disturbances. He'd assured her he'd keep the kids occupied downstairs and hinted at taking them to the park for a spell.

"A little surprise for you." Reed grinned.

He looked mighty pleased with himself, but she couldn't imagine what he must have gone through to prepare the meal while wrangling two little ones. "Brielle was worried you'd sit up here and starve, so we made you breakfast. She saw this on one of those YouTube channels she watches."

Brielle was obsessed with watching two little girls who had a YouTube channel. Mostly she watched them play with dolls, but the girls also went on excursions to the park and interacted with their family. She often wanted to duplicate whatever she saw them do.

Reed set the tray across her lap and dropped a kiss to her lips. Meanwhile, Brielle helped her little brother onto the bed and then climbed up herself.

"We helped Daddy make breakfast," Brielle said.

"Yeah, they did," Reed said dryly.

"You did? Thank you, sweetie." Anika bit back a smile and kissed Brielle's cheek. She knew from experience how much coordination it took to manage both kids while trying to prepare a meal with their so-called help.

Anika carefully placed the orange juice on the table beside the bed. "Oh my goodness, look at these pancakes." Three heart-shaped pancakes with bacon, scrambled eggs, and fruit sat on the plate.

"Daddy made those with a special mold," Brielle explained.

"Your daddy is very creative," Anika said.

Her son touched the bacon on the plate. "Mommy."

"That's right, bacon. Food of the gods." Anika tapped his nose.

Her son laughed, as if she'd said the funniest thing in the

world. Adopting him to round out their family had been an easy decision. She and Reed had seen the photos of him and fallen in love. The icing on the cake had been finalizing her adoption of Brielle on the same day.

"Come here, my beautiful boy. Mwah, mwah." She dropped sloppy kisses on his cheek, and he squirmed, giggling happily.

"I love bacon, too," Brielle announced.

"I know you do. Come here, my beautiful girl." Anika pulled Brielle into a hug and delivered the same number of sloppy kisses, listening to her daughter squeal.

Her arms were not only filled with her kids, her heart was as well. Across the room, Reed snapped photos of them.

"Stop, honey." Anika self-consciously smoothed her hair. She didn't have on a stitch of makeup.

"I took some good candid shots," he said.

"I'm sure I look awful."

His affection for her was evident in his eyes. "You look beautiful."

"At least take one with me looking at the camera. We'll pose for it."

"All right. Everybody get in position."

Anika set the food on the floor and they rearranged on the bed. Jaden stood with an arm around her neck. Brielle snuggled close with both arms around Anika's waist, her cheek to Anika's breast, and smiling at the camera.

"Perfect," Reed said.

After snapping a few photos and showing them to Anika for her approval, he started herding the kids out of the room. "Okay, let's go people." He scooped up Jaden. "Let's leave mommy alone so she can have some quiet time. Remember, today's her day."

Jaden stuck his thumb in his mouth, his eyes big and pitiful as he looked over his father's shoulder at Anika. Brielle pouted but slid off the bed.

"It's okay, they can stay," Anika said, as they shuffled toward the door.

Reed paused halfway across the floor. "You sure about that?"

She looked at her kids and her husband. Over two years of marriage and this was her first official Mother's Day. This one, at least, she didn't want to spend alone. She wanted to be with her family, the people she loved and who loved her. No matter how crazy or noisy or boisterous the day turned out to be.

"Yes, it's okay."

"Yay!" Brielle said. She started dancing around the room. Reed placed Jaden on the bed, who immediately became caught up in his sister's excitement and jumped up and down on the mattress.

Reed sat beside Anika and kept an eye on the kids. "You sure? Because just so you know, I'm taking my day on Father's Day."

Anika put an arm around his neck and pulled him backward so his head rested on the pillow beside her. "I'm sure."

"Okay, Jaden, that's enough, son," Reed said. The little boy stopped immediately and fell out on the bed as if he'd done a day's work in those few minutes.

"Let's see, we have a dancer slash opera singer, and what appears to be an actor."

Reed chuckled. "We're going to be well taken care of in our old age."

"I think so, too."

"Hey."

Anika looked into Reed's blue eyes. He smiled, but she saw seriousness there, too.

He ran his thumb across her bottom lip. "I love you."

Her heart tightened with bliss. At times she still couldn't believe that she had been blessed enough to marry this man and share raising these wonderful, loud, sticky-fingered children with him.

"I love you, too."

LOVE UNEXPECTED SERIES

Check out the entire Love Unexpected series and fall in love with Ryan and Shawna, Tomas and Talia, Jay and Brenda, Ransom and Sophie, Diego and Ronnie, and Reed and Anika in The Blind Date, The Wrong Man, An Unexpected Attraction, The Right Time, One of the Guys, and That Time in Venice.

Hawthorne Family series

- The Temptation of a Good Man
- A Hard Man to Love
- Here Comes Trouble
- For Better or Worse
- Hawthorne Family Series: Vol. I (print anthology)
- Hawthorne Family Series: Vol. II (print anthology)

Bailar series (sweet/clean romance)

- Worth Waiting For

Stand Alones

- A Passionate Love
- Passion Rekindled
- Still in Love
- Subordinate Position
- Heartbreak in Rio (part of Endless Summer Nights)

Free Stories: www.delaneydiamond.com

ABOUT THE AUTHOR

Delaney Diamond is the USA Today Bestselling Author of sweet, sensual, passionate romance novels. Originally from the U.S. Virgin Islands, she now lives in Atlanta, Georgia. She reads romance novels, mysteries, thrillers, and a fair amount of nonfiction. When she's not busy reading or writing, she's in the kitchen trying out new recipes, dining at one of her favorite restaurants, or traveling to an interesting locale.

Enjoy free reads and the first chapter of all her novels on her website. Join her mailing list to get sneak peeks, notices of sale prices, and find out about new releases.

www.delaneydiamond.com

CPSIA information can be obtained
at www.ICGtesting.com
Printed in the USA
LVOW11s1504141217
559732LV00001B/59/P